CASEY AND THE LOST BOYS

As DI Casey Clunes investigates the whereabouts of a missing volunteer, the suspicious behaviour of a group of schoolboys begins to interrupt not only her work, but her home life too . . . In *The Other Diana*, a teacher reveals a long-kept secret, leading to the re-opening of a twenty-year-old unsolved case involving a murdered girl . . . And in *After Phoebe*, Vonny is forced to take a job at Oxford University and confront the darkness of her past. But now, she feels the presence of something far more threatening than her memories . . .

GERALDINE RYAN

CASEY AND THE LOST BOYS

Complete and Unabridged

LINFORD
Leicester

First published in Great Britain

First Linford Edition
published 2019

A catalogue record for this book is available
from the British Library.

ISBN 978–1–4448–4300–2

Published by
F. A. Thorpe (Publishing)
Anstey, Leicestershire

Set by Words & Graphics Ltd.
Anstey, Leicestershire
Printed and bound in Great Britain by
T. J. International Ltd., Padstow, Cornwall

This book is printed on acid-free paper

Casey and the Lost Boys

1

Casey knew something was up as soon as she got inside the house. Usually, when Finlay came in from school and Dom came back from wherever he'd been that day, they both dropped their stuff on the floor for her to trip over. But tonight, everything had been neatly hung up and put away. She stared suspiciously at their outdoor shoes, sitting innocently side by side. It took her by surprise how Finlay's were almost as big as Dom's. When did her little boy get to be so big?

Oscar, their chocolate-coloured spaniel, wandered out of the kitchen to greet her. She put out a hand and patted his head absentmindedly before cautiously making her way into the kitchen, Oscar snuffling at her heels. The smell of cooking raised her suspicions even further. Dom was a better cook than she was, probably because working from home meant he got most practice. But time-keeping had never been his strong point. This had to be one of the few times he'd ever promised dinner at seven and actually had it ready on time.

He was doling out something stew-like onto three plates. Finlay was already at the table, eagerly scanning his plate to make sure he wasn't being short-changed. Time was when he would have jumped up and put his arms round her and given her a big sloppy kiss. She told herself not to be sentimental. At very nearly twelve years old he was growing up and growing away from her. Wasn't that how it was supposed to be?

'I thought that was you, love,' Dom said, pausing briefly in his task.

'Well, I *am* the only other person with a key to this place,' she said.

'So far,' Finlay muttered.

A glance passed between father and son that she couldn't interpret.

'Come and sit down,' Dom said, taking his seat. 'You'll be hungry after your shift. It's pork and pepper casserole. Your favourite.'

There was a definite nervous edge to

Dom's voice. Now she was certain there was something going on. The dinner smelled good. But there was another smell in the room that was a good deal stronger. The smell of rat.

'OK,' she said. 'Can we drop the Stepford husband act, Dom? It's not really your style.'

Dom, his eyes fixed on his meal, pushed his food around the plate like a man who'd suddenly discovered he had no appetite.

'Finlay? Perhaps you'll enlighten me,' she said.

Finlay loaded rice onto his fork. It was nothing to do with him, he announced, and anyway, hadn't she always said that if ever you did something stupid then you should be man enough to own up to it. Since he'd started secondary school, Finlay had an answer for everything, she mused.

'Okay.' Dom put down his fork. 'I should have said no. Or at least said I needed to discuss it with you first,' he said. 'But they needed an answer right then and they're two of my oldest friends.'

Casey sat down and waited for the explanation. She'd been across a table from enough criminals to know that once they had something on their mind, sooner or later they'd feel compelled to spill the beans. Not that Dom was a criminal. He just looked guilty.

But it was Finlay who was the first to crack. 'There's this boy,' he said. 'He's in Year Eleven and halfway through his GCSE course. Dad said he could come and live here while his parents went off to Africa for six months.'

'What?'

It was worse than she'd thought!

'They're aid workers and there's some sort of crisis. And he wouldn't be able to do his GCSEs where they're going,' Finlay went on.

Aid workers? Who did they know who were aid workers? The Renshaws, of course. Liz and Chris. Dom had been at university with both of them, which meant they all three went back a long, long way. They were good people with strong principles. The kind of good people that made everyone else look bad.

She stared at her plate while all sorts of objections ran through her head as to why she didn't want some fifteen-year-old boy sleeping in her spare room for the next six months. A boy she'd only ever met about three times in her life and who'd barely said a word on all three occasions. She didn't think she'd recognise him if she passed him in the street. In fact, she couldn't even remember his name.

'See, I said she wouldn't be too pleased,' Finlay said.

That was an understatement if ever there was one.

'They wouldn't have asked if they hadn't been so desperate,' Dom said. 'And they're needed out there.'

She stabbed a piece of pepper with her fork. Of course they were needed out there. How very clever of Dom to mention it. Now, if she put her foot down she'd make them look even more worthy, while ensuring she came across as a selfish, over-privileged harpy.

'Well if you've already agreed then I don't suppose there's any point in me objecting,' she said.

Relief flooded Dom's face. 'You don't mind?'

'I didn't say that,' she said.

Finlay chuckled.

'So when can we expect him?' she said.

'He's down to start at St Bede's after half term,' Dom said. 'Luckily they're covering the same syllabus there as in his old school. And it means that at least he'll know Finlay.'

'Leave me out of it,' Finlay muttered, darkly. 'I'd prefer to choose my own friends if it's all the same to you.'

Casey chewed the piece of pepper thoughtfully, while simultaneously digesting Dom's news.

'That means you've got a week to clear out the spare room and get it ready for him,' she said, once she'd swallowed both.

If Dom thought she was going to let him off the hook so easily, then he had several things coming.

★ ★ ★

Casey was glad to get to work the next day. It meant there was less time to dwell on the prospect of Giles Renshaw coming to stay. Six months was a long time to

8

play surrogate parents to a surly teenager. At least, she presumed he'd be surly, given what she'd heard about teenagers from friends who had their own. Heaven only knew how much of Giles' surliness would rub off on Finlay, too. That boy of hers had always shown himself to be a quick learner.

St Anthony's Church, or rather the ugly modern extension stuck on the back of the church, was Casey's destination this afternoon. Tony's, as it was called, was a drop-in centre for anyone down on their luck. It had been running for ten years now, limping along with financial hand-outs from the parish and the council, with the occasional bequest from those towns-people with a social conscience.

One of the volunteers, Arlan Roberts, had disappeared without letting any of the other volunteers know where he was going. They'd waited a fortnight before reporting it. But when calls to his mobile continued to go unanswered, Julie Martin, who ran the centre, had begun to grow increasingly concerned.

It was she who'd contacted Casey's

private number a couple of days previously. She hadn't wanted to make his disappearance official, she'd said, because after all, Arlan was a grown man and entitled to come and go as he pleased. Plus, as a volunteer nobody expected him to turn up every day.

But on the other hand, she'd added, he would never not turn up if he'd promised to come in. So if Casey could pop round in her lunch hour some time, she'd be really grateful. Since Casey hadn't seen Julie in a long while, she decided it would be good to catch up, even if, in the interim, this Arlan Roberts had shown up.

When they'd first met, Casey had been a young DC. Julie's adopted daughter Rose had been a troubled adolescent. In those days Julie was always at the police station, arriving to collect Rose and take her home after whatever misdemeanour had landed her in custody this time. Casey and Julie had become quite close, with Casey always ready to lend a sympathetic ear whenever Julie needed to offload her concerns and fears for Rose.

It turned out that Julie had good cause

to be concerned. Rose took up with an older man — a dealer — and had a child with him. She turned to substance abuse when he upped and left her to bring their baby up on her own. Social Services would have taken the child away had Julie not stepped in. Rose had taken off then, and Julie had raised her grandson single-handedly ever since.

Casey would have admired Julie for this alone. But it was the calm way she tolerated Rose's extreme behaviour that had made her admire her even more. Rose has had a bad start in life, was all Julie would ever say, even when Rose stole from her and, once or twice, even attacked her. She believed that she could save her daughter through love alone. Casey, more cynical, had always doubted it. She wondered what Rose was up to now? She certainly wasn't living in Brockhaven or the police would surely know about it!

During the course of one week, Tony's underwent many transformations. It was a food bank, a soup kitchen, an outpost of Citizens Advice. Young carers met here one afternoon a week after school, to let their hair down briefly before resuming their caring roles. The one constant however was the Community café that provided cheap food and hot drinks at highly subsidised prices for those on low incomes.

Lunchtime was over now and only one or two customers remained. There was a smell of stale food in the air and the clatter of dishes from the kitchen drowned the cheerful chatter of the women volunteers as they tackled the washing up. At first, Casey didn't recognise the woman wiping a cloth over a table. But when she turned round she realised it was Julie.

'Casey? Is it really you?'

She'd got thinner, Casey couldn't help noticing, and there were dark shadows, like bruises, under her eyes. She'd be — what — 60 now? By her reckoning, Johnny, Rose's son, would be a teenager. It couldn't have been easy looking after a grandson at an age when many of her friends would be looking forward to having the house to themselves again.

'It's not bad news is it?' Julie said.

Casey quickly reassured her. She was

just here to find out more about the man who'd gone missing, she said.

'And I thought it would be nice to see you too,' she said. 'It's been a while. How are you?'

'I'm good,' Julie said, overly brightly, Casey thought.

'And how's Johnny? He must be — what — fourteen now?'

'Fifteen,' Julie said. 'He's at St Bede's.'

'Oh, like my boy,' Casey said. 'I expect he keeps you busy,' she added, brightly.

A weak smile was Julie's only response. Julie was giving off the sort of vibes that told her any more questions would be prying. Or maybe she was just imagining it and Julie was simply a very busy woman.

'So,' she said. 'Tell me about Arlan.'

'Come along to the kitchen and I'll tell you everything while I make us both a cuppa.'

⋆ ⋆ ⋆

When Casey returned to the station some two hours later, there were half a dozen officers gathered in the staff kitchen, some still togged up in their stab vests. By the look of it, they'd not long got back from a skirmish.

'What have I missed, Jimmy?' Casey said to Jimmy Wyatt, who'd not long qualified and who appeared to have come off second in an exchange of blows.

According to Jimmy, a disagreement had started in Starbucks in the High Street between two local families, the Daleys and the Stocks, both well-known for their fiery tempers and probably responsible for 80% of local crime. The argument, apparently, had quickly turned into a fight, spilling out onto the street. No doubt it was the adrenaline the situation had demanded of them that accounted for her colleagues' high spirits.

'I hope you made a few arrests,' she said.

Only last week they'd had a round robin email in which the Super had informed them that they were bottom of the county league table when it came to the number of arrests they'd made that month. They were all going to have to pull their socks up, had been the implication.

'Can't speak for the others,' he said. 'But I made my first.'

'Congratulations! Let's hope you can make it stick,' she said, as she by-passed the group to get to the Super's office. 'Oh, and I'd put some ice on that,' she said, as a parting shot.

★   ★   ★

Superintendent Jess Morgan studied the photo of Arlan Roberts that Casey had presented her with for a long while, before she finally spoke.

'This hipster beard thing,' she said. 'What's it all about, Casey?'

Casey said she didn't know. But it seemed to be turning into an epidemic. The Super nodded in agreement. One of her nephews had grown one, she said. He'd asked for something called beard oil for Christmas, apparently. She'd sent him a book token instead.

'Anyway, never mind him. Tell me about your missing man,' she said.

15

Casey recited the information she'd been presented with.

'He's 34. Not local. Turned up one day six months ago asking if he could volunteer at Tony's. They were desperate. He's been there ever since.'

'What's his background?'

'Julie remembers him saying he came from Surrey. Some big house, nice middle class family. Dad expected him to get a job in a bank like he did himself but apparently that's not his style.'

'A do-gooder.'

It wasn't a question.

'Have they tried to find him?' the Super said. 'Been to his flat?'

'Nobody knows where he lives. Apparently he sofa surfs,' Casey said. 'I mean, he's not getting paid for what he does so he won't be able to afford rent.'

'What about phoning his parents in Surrey?'

'She's done that too,' Casey said. 'First couple of times she just rang off when nobody replied. But since then she's left messages. She wonders if they might have gone on holiday.'

The Super considered this.

'Julie's rung him countless times too, of course. Left messages on his mobile. But to no avail. That's why she rang me in the end,' Casey said. 'Plus on the last day she spoke to him, he promised to turn up the next day to help at the food bank.'

'And he didn't.'

'Correct.'

Casey was getting the distinct impression that the Super wasn't particularly interested in supplying officers to look for a sofa-surfing, middle-class hipster who said one thing and did another. She'd have thought the same herself. Except Julie was a good judge of character. If she was worried, then it wouldn't be for no reason.

'I'm not sure we've got the manpower to expend on this, Casey,' she said.

So she was right then!

'There was another brawl this afternoon.'

'But that was just a spat, surely, between the Stocks and the Daleys?' Casey said. 'You know what they're like.'

'More than most,' the Super admitted. 'But I'm worried it might escalate. You've heard those rumours about London gangs coming down here looking for new markets.'

'I've heard. But I haven't seen any evidence.'

'Maybe that's because you haven't been looking hard enough.'

What on earth was that supposed to mean, Casey wondered.

'I think your skills would be much better used keeping your ear to the ground and trying to find out who it is that wants to turn our lovely little seaside town of Brockhaven into a dealer's paradise,' she said. 'And as far Arlan Robertson is concerned . . . '

'Roberts,' said Casey, correcting her.

The Super smiled. 'As for Mr Roberts, I suggest you ask this Julie to get in touch with Missing People. If anyone can find him, they can.'

★   ★   ★

To say Casey was in a bad mood right now would have been a huge understatement. It was half past midnight and tomorrow she had an early morning meeting with the Outreach team, the purpose of which was to identify anyone who might be an easy target for any out-of-town gang looking to find a market for their drugs here in Brockhaven.

At a guess that would be ten percent of the population. First of all, there were the addicts, who'd think their Christmases had all come at once if someone offered to pay them in drugs just to run a few 'errands'. Then there were the desperate, who needed the money for food and in order to pay their rent. And the avaricious, who'd risk prison just for the shiny things their ill-gotten gains could provide them with. That was just for starters. But it was the ambitious ones who were the most dangerous. Because they got greedy and competitive and before long you found yourself policing a turf war. It didn't bear thinking about.

Casey was making up the spare bed. It was a task she could have done without but the Renshaws had left them with little choice. She hadn't asked for the details on the phone — frankly, she hadn't wanted them — but they had to leave for Africa immediately, which meant that from tonight Giles would be homeless. Of course, they could drive him round right away, she heard herself saying.

So now the poor boy hovered in the doorway, waiting for her to finish her task. Her first impression of him had been of a tall, skinny, awkward looking boy with floppy hair and legs that went on forever. So far he'd said little but please and thank you. He'd apologised a great deal too. So much so that Casey couldn't help feeling sorry for him. None of this was his fault after all. She made a silent vow to make more of an effort with him.

If she was annoyed with anyone it was the Super, for landing her with a job she didn't want. She was annoyed with herself too for having to ring up Julie and tell her she didn't think that Arlan going missing was a priority right now.

If Julie had called her out on it she wouldn't have felt so bad. But she'd been so understanding. She'd apologised for making a fuss and insisted she understood about priorities. She'd even welcomed the speed with which Casey had got back to her.

'Right, Giles,' she said, summoning all her cheerfulness. 'I'll leave you to it. Sweet dreams.'

He gave an awkward smile and once more thanked her politely. Tomorrow he could sleep in. The school weren't expecting him for another three days anyway, so there was no need to get him up for breakfast. Once he'd woken up she'd let Dom deal with him for the rest of the day.

Needing some alone time Casey crept downstairs and into the kitchen where she fixed herself a whisky. It always worked far better for her than hot chocolate. When her phone rang she assumed it would be one of the Renshaws, asking after Giles. But it was Julie. And she sounded worried.

'I'm sorry to ring you so late Casey,' she said. 'I was going to leave it till tomorrow. But I don't think I'll get a wink of sleep unless I share what I've just learned.'

'Go on.'

Casey took a sip of whisky. The alcohol burned her throat, but not unpleasantly.

'I got a call from the number Arlan gave me.'

'His parents' number? They're back from holiday, then.'

There was a long pause. Casey thought the phone had died on her. But then Julie spoke again.

'This is the thing, Casey. The man I spoke to, the one I assumed was Arlan's father. Well — he told me that Arlan had been dead these last three years.'

2

It was early the next morning and Casey was back at Tony's.

'Honestly, Casey,' Julie said. 'I'm still shaken up about it. I was on my way to bed for the night when I got his call.'

'And he definitely said his name was John Roberts and he was the father of Arlan?'

Julie nodded earnestly. 'Very well spoken. Sort of commanding, you know.'

She puffed out her chest as she launched into what Casey could only imagine was an impression of the man.

' 'Is this some sort of joke?' he says. 'Because if so, then it's in very poor taste.' Honestly, I didn't know where to put myself,' she went on.

Casey's phone beeped a message. She chose to ignore it. It was bound to be from the Super asking why she wasn't at her meeting. To Casey's mind, that meeting was nothing but a PR thing — an opportunity for the Super to display Brockhaven Constabulary's social conscience to the town worthies. And to put on record that, should any violence break out on the estates further down the line, the Super could never be accused of lack of foresight. Jess Morgan might wear the navy blue uniform of a chief superintendent, but underneath the shiny buttons, she was a politician through and through.

'Get that if you want,' Julie said.

'It's not important,' Casey said. 'Go on with your story.'

Julie closed her eyes briefly, putting herself back inside last night's conversation with the man who insisted he was Arlan Roberts' father.

'So after I apologise for all the messages I've left, that's when he tells me Arlan died three years ago. Cancer.'

'Did he tell you what date?'

Julie pulled a face. 'I think so. But I can't remember. I was just so shocked.'

'It doesn't matter,' Casey reassured her.

'I do remember he said that Arlan had been twenty-eight though. Does that help?'

'Greatly,' said Casey.

It didn't, but she hated to see Julie so disappointed.

'Did Arlan — or the guy who said he was Arlan — give you any legal documents to prove he was who he said he was?' Casey asked.

'Well, no. Normally I'd get references and that, but this was just a few hours a week as and when.' She bit her lip and looked at the floor. 'Will I get into bother?'

'What do you mean? What for?'

'I don't know. Maybe I should have had a police check done on him,' she said. 'But we were desperate for help.'

She could always muster enough volunteers among the women in the Parish, she explained. But strong, young men who could lift boxes full of tins for the food bank and help the buggies up and down the steps were like gold dust. When he turned up out of the blue it was as if her prayers had been answered.

Casey reassured Julie that she wasn't in any trouble. A man had gone missing and she'd reported it. It was just bad luck he

25

hadn't turned out to be the person he'd said he was. If only they had any sort of idea about where he lived they could pay a visit to his place of residence; find something with his DNA on it and have it analysed. Then, if he was on their system, he could be identified.

'Do you mean he might be a criminal?' Julie said, suddenly horror-struck at the thought that she'd been employing someone with a record in a position of trust.

'Not necessarily,' Casey said. 'But if he's ever been arrested — even wrongly — we'll have a sample of his DNA.'

Julie looked thoughtful. 'Can you wait a minute?' she said.

'What's up?'

She'd suddenly remembered, she said. She'd got one of Arlan's shirts.

'How come?'

'He'd lost some buttons. Two from the sleeves. A couple from the front. I said I'd remove all of them and replace them with a new set.'

'Really?'

Casey didn't think she'd ever sewn a button on a man's shirt in her entire life.

'And you've still got the shirt?'

Julie nodded. It was in her locker. In a plastic bag. She kept forgetting to take it home, she said.

'Let's go and get it then,' Casey said. 'See if we can't find out Arlan Roberts' true identity.'

* * *

By the time Casey had driven over to the forensics lab and deposited the shirt, rung the Station to arrange for the police over in Sussex to pay a call on John Roberts, and driven over to the Super's meeting, which was being held in the Guildhall, she discovered she'd missed it by a good twenty minutes.

It probably hadn't helped that she'd taken a bit of a detour. She'd tried to ignore her conscience but in the end she'd felt compelled to drive home to check on their new resident. Giles Renshaw wasn't her responsibility. Dom was perfectly capable of looking after the boy — if he even *needed* looking after, for God's sake. He was sixteen! Well, almost.

And if he wanted anything, then he had a tongue in his head, surely?

But he was in a strange house, in a strange town, about to be thrown into a strange school. And if that had been her boy, well — wouldn't she have wished for someone to make him feel as much at home as if he were in his own house with his own family?

When she got home, however, the house was empty apart from Dom, who was sitting enjoying a cup of coffee while he read the morning paper, Oscar at his feet. Apparently Giles had been keen to start at St Bede's immediately, so Dom had fed him toast, made a quick call to the boy's year tutor to check that it was okay, then jumped in the car to drive him over there.

'It was his choice, Casey' Dom said defensively, when Casey questioned his decision to fall in so easily with Giles' wishes. 'What was I supposed to do? Lock him in his room?'

She hadn't had time for an argument so she'd left it there and got back in the car. But she couldn't help feeling they'd failed the boy at the first hurdle. Dom could have offered him an alternative to school today — a walk with Oscar, or a trip out to point out the area's places of interest, for example.

That's what she'd have done. That way she'd have got him to open up a bit more about himself than he'd done already. Found out how he was really feeling. It was all right Dom insisting that Giles was really keen to start school today. But maybe he was just being brave and inside he was terrified.

Damn the boy, she thought, as she arrived at the Station and parked in the one remaining parking space. Hadn't she said having a teenager in the house would be a bad idea?

★　★　★

He stood with his back to the railings, affecting a nonchalant stance. Mid-morning break. How long was it? Fifteen minutes? He just had to endure it for another ten, then he could go back inside and hide at his desk — till lunchtime, when he'd have

29

to go through the humiliation of not knowing where to go or what to do once more,
but this time for a full hour.

At least this school was mixed, unlike
his last one. A couple of the girls had said
hello already, one had even spoken and
said if there was anything he wanted to
know, then he should just ask her. Not
that he had any intentions of doing that.
He didn't have the nerve. But perhaps if
he had, he wouldn't be standing here
now, like Billy No-Mates.

They were over there, those girls, heads
together, deep in conversation. Were they
talking about him? Discussing what a
loser he was? Giles got out his phone and
pretended to read his messages. Of course
he didn't have any. Mum and Dad were
probably still on a plane. Even if they'd
finally arrived at their destination, there
wouldn't be any Wi-Fi. They only ever
went to places where the mod-cons were
dodgy, if they even existed at all. It was
like convenience was anathema to them.

His eye was drawn to two boys up near
the bike shed, half-hidden by all the bikes.
He got a sense that there was something

going on between them. Something bad that he couldn't put his finger on. One of the boys was bigger than the other. He towered over the smaller one, occasionally prodding him with a finger. Every time he did so, the smaller, skinnier boy shrank back. But because of all the bikes there was nowhere else to go. He was cornered.

He put his phone away and started to walk in their direction. Quietly, so as not to alert them. It was none of his business but Giles couldn't help himself. Whatever this was, he wasn't going to stand there and watch it happen without trying to do something about it.

He couldn't have been watching where he was going because he walked straight into a bike wheel, his shin colliding sharply with the edge of the back mudguard, causing him to cry out in pain. The boys' heads turned towards him, simultaneously. The bigger boy dropped his grip on the smaller boy's jumper. It was an opportunity for the smaller one to wriggle out of his corner and compose himself.

'What do you want?' the bigger boy said, sharply.

His accent was rough and he looked hard. Boys like that were good at fighting because they didn't care if they got hurt. They were too stupid. This was both an advantage and a disadvantage to boys like Giles.

'Are you ok?' he said to the smaller one, ignoring the other one's question.

The boy sniffed, rubbed his nose, and glanced up warily at his bully. But he said nothing.

'Just do one, will you?' the bigger boy said. 'This is a private conversation.'

Giles continued to ignore him.

'Is he bothering you?' he asked again.

With another cursory glance at his captor the smaller boy replied that no, he wasn't.

'You heard him,' the bigger boy said. 'And you heard me. Now get lost.'

He had no idea what to do, now that his offer of rescue had been spurned not once, but twice. But Giles stood his ground. Fortunately for him, just when he didn't think he could keep it up for much longer, the bell rang.

He felt almost triumphant when the

bigger of the two boys moved first. He edged his way out of the bike shed and began to walk in the direction of the school entrance. Giles kept his eyes fastened on the smaller boy. He prayed he was doing the right thing by not moving. He had his back toward the bigger boy, which made him vulnerable. But to show fear made him a victim. Just like this other boy was.

'Remember what I said.'

The bully's words as he walked away were directed at his target, Giles assumed.

'Don't let me down,' he added, tossing the words nonchalantly over his shoulder as he strolled away.

It was just the two of them now, and a few other stragglers making their way reluctantly inside.

'Look,' Giles said.

He was about to offer the boy his support. Tell him that if he felt he was being bullied he should report it. But he didn't get a chance.

'Stay away from me,' the boy said, almost spitting out his words. 'I can look after myself.'

And with that he ran off towards his bully, catching him up at the school entrance. Had he got it wrong, Giles wondered. Was this just a bit of banter? A friendly argument between two good mates? He'd have liked to think so. But somehow he didn't think it was.

★　★　★

Julie watched Casey's car pull away. She hadn't stayed that long in the end because she had to get to some meeting or other. It was clear she hadn't really wanted to go to it though and Julie was sorry she had to leave. More than ever, she needed someone to talk to. Casey had been a great listener in the past, when she'd had her problems with Rose. Now, she thought, it was happening all over again — but this time with Johnny.

She'd had her suspicions for a while. He'd always been so open with her. But now he was — well, there was no other word for it — furtive. He'd let himself in after school and not even bother to call out hello before disappearing into his room. The other evening she'd gone up there to tell him his tea was ready and when she knocked on the door there was no reply. Twice more she'd knocked and still got no answer. So she'd let herself into his room, only to find it empty. He must have slipped out the front way while she'd been in the kitchen getting the tea ready.

Some instinct from the past sent her over to his chest of drawers. When Rose had lived here she'd hide her drugs inside her balled up socks. Julie would find other things there too. Stuff she'd stolen — make up, jewellery, money from Julie's purse. Once, a pregnancy test.

All the time she was looking she held her breath, praying she wouldn't find anything that might incriminate Johnny. How could she ever bear going through all that again? When all she found were the folded up T-shirts, socks and under-pants that you'd expect to find in a young boy's chest of drawers she felt almost delirious with happiness. This was good, kind, straightforward little Johnny, not Rose with all her complications. There was nothing to worry about with him.

But then she'd gone to pick up a jumper he'd left lying on the floor. She took it over to the wardrobe to hang it up. That's when she saw that white shoe box. Don't look inside she'd told herself. Don't. Because if you do, you might see something that will change everything. She should have listened to herself. But instead she'd reached down, picked up the box and opened the lid. Inside was a brand new pair of trainers. And inside one of the trainers was a bundle of ten pound notes.

She stared at the contents of the box for a long time, growing gradually more numb with shock. It was as if her present life had been lifted up then dropped right back inside the same room, fifteen years earlier. Back then, when she'd first realised what Rose was getting into into, she'd reacted the only way she knew how. Furiously.

She'd thrown the book at her, grounding her, watching her like a hawk, even going so far as accompanying her to school and collecting her at the end of every school day. If she'd imagined that her methods would work, she quickly learned her lesson. It was inevitable that Rose would rebel in the face of such a harsh regime.

With Johnny, she would do things differently. When she got home this evening she'd talk to him. Quietly. Calmly. She'd choose her words carefully. She'd get him back before he'd even properly pulled away. She wasn't going to lose this one.

★　★　★

During her phone call with Sergeant Mike Charnley, Casey had learned a lot about Arlan Roberts. According to the local bobby, who'd just got back from interviewing the deceased man's father, he'd been the perfect son — the apple of his parents' eye.

Understandably, his father, John, was still upset from Julie's phone call. Never a day went by without him and his wife grieving over their loss. To think that someone had been impersonating Arlan all these months — longer, for all they knew — was beyond distressing.

Casey and the Sergeant had very quickly got onto first name terms — summed up the real Arlan Roberts very quickly. He'd been a bright, middle-class, privately educated boy with the kind of conventional path that had been laid out before him by a long line of previous generations. Namely university and then a career in banking or the law. But Arlan had had other ideas. He'd wanted to paint and had gone off to art school. It was no use his parents trying to persuade him otherwise. Arlan was Arlan and he'd made up his mind.

They'd wanted to buy him a flat apparently, once he'd finished his degree and it became apparent that he was never going to be able to make much of a living from his art. But he'd refused and had taken up squatting instead.

'He just wasn't interested in making money,' so John Roberts had told Mike. 'He wanted to do what he could to make the world a better place. And I suppose he did, in his own small way.'

His own small way, according to what Mike told her, was using his art to help turn people's lives round. Before he became too ill to carry on he gave Art classes in Lumbley Gaol, a rambling old Victorian prison somewhere in the north of England.

Casey sat at her desk mulling over what she'd just been told, wondering where this new information would take her next, if anywhere at all. The real Arlan Roberts had led an unconventional kind of life and must have met some unconventional people on his journey. Was the man who'd stolen his name one of them? Or had he simply glimpsed it on a headstone one day when he'd been taking a walk through a Surrey graveyard?

She wished people would stop coming in and out. Every time the door opened, she was certain that the next person to come in would be the Super, arriving to rip her into humiliating shreds in front of everyone for her no-show earlier. But the next person turned out to be the Desk Sergeant. Someone was waiting for her in the outer office. A woman — could she speak to her?

As soon as she set eyes on the small, slim woman who perched awkwardly on a chair by the entrance, clutching her hand-bag on her lap, Casey realised she recognised her from somewhere. The woman leapt out of her seat and came towards her. Her name was Maggie Fowler, she said. She was a volunteer at Tony's. Of course, Casey had glimpsed her there, when she'd been making her initial call.

She hadn't wanted to say anything earlier, when Casey had been talking to Julie because she didn't want to upset Julie, she said.

'Why would Julie be upset, Mrs Fowler?' Casey said.

'Miss,' Maggie replied. 'It's Miss Fowler.'

Casey apologised. She really wasn't inter-ested in Maggie's marital status. She just wanted her to get on with it. Whatever she had to say it was clearly a real challenge for her to get the words out. Casey waited patiently. It was all she could do in the circumstances.

'I've seen them twice over the last fortnight. Arguing. He looked frightened. Arlan did. I mean, the one we all thought was Arlan.'

'Who, Maggie?'

'It looked like he was threatening him. His final day. Julie had gone home. They were in the ginnel that cuts through between the church and my estate. He looked terrified.'

'Who was threatening whom?' Casey said.

'Arlan didn't come back the next day. He hasn't been back since. I think he's run away. To try to get away from him. Because he's a bad lot that one and he always will be.'

Please God, Casey silently prayed, show me the way here.

'Who was threatening the man you knew as Arlan?' she said. 'Who was he running away from?'

'It was Steve Parr,' Maggie said. 'That's why I was scared to say anything until now. I didn't want to upset Julie. Not after everything she's gone through with her Rose and all that.'

Steve Parr was Johnny's father. Julie's son-in-law. Back on the scene after all these years. No wonder Maggie Fowler wanted to keep that information away from Julie. When her phone rang she

41

fumbled in her pocket for it. It was Debbie, from Forensics.

'Hi, Casey,' she said cheerfully. 'I thought you might like to know. We've got a name for you. We've discovered the true identity of your missing man.'

3

The name David Lyall, passed on to her from Debbie, her contact at Forensics, had initially meant nothing to Casey. Fortunately, when she ran it through the PNC, the computer revealed everything she needed to know. He had a record as long as her arm and had been in and out of prison for much of his adult life.

Running her eye down the long list of his offences, she lost count of the number of times she read the word 'burglary'. He'd also been done for handling stolen goods, going equipped to steal and — most interestingly to Casey, given what Maggie Fowler had told her about seeing Lyall deep in conversation with Steve Parr — assisting offenders.

Maggie had reported that there'd been some very noticeable friction between Lyall and Parr when she'd spotted them deep in conversation the afternoon before Lyall disappeared from Tony's, where he'd been volunteering. She said he'd looked scared of Parr. It occurred to Casey that Parr might have some sort of hold over Lyall. What had been the purpose of his visit? Somehow Casey didn't see it as merely a social one. Did Lyall owe him a favour and Parr had come to collect it?

According to the PNC, the last time David Lyall had been in prison was for a period between January 2012 and April 2013. Since his release he seemed to have stayed on the straight and narrow. Volunteering at Tony's would suggest that he'd turned his life completely around, which was never easy to do. So fair play to him, thought Casey.

It was only a guess, but Casey imagined that Lyall must have first encountered Steve Parr before he went straight. If Lyall, who'd changed his life round, had been reluctant to renew his relationship with Parr, fearful of where it might lead him again, then that would certainly explain his desire to get as far away from him as possible.

A few more clicks of the mouse satisfied Casey's curiosity. And then, eureka! She had the Arlan Roberts connection too! At the very moment everything suddenly became clear, who should stick her head round the door but the Super? Casey swore inwardly. All day long she'd been glancing over her shoulder wondering when Jess Morgan was going to pounce on her to say something about her having missed her meeting this morning.

She'd heard all about it anyway from someone else who'd been there. And just as she'd predicted she'd missed nothing. Like most meetings it was just another excuse for everyone to get very aerated. She could pretty much guarantee that by this time next week everything would have subsided into exactly the same state it was before the meeting.

It was typical that just as she'd let her guard slip for five minutes the Super had managed to sneak up on her. If only she'd shown up ten minutes later Casey would have been in her car and driving home.

'There you are!'

The Super was braced for confrontation. There was only one thing for Casey to do now and that was to bluff her way out of trouble.

'I've been trying to find you all day,' she went on.

Casey thanked her colleagues silently for keeping their word and not giving away her whereabouts. She decided to land a pre-emptive strike.

'I thought you might like to know that Steve Parr's back in Brockhaven,' she said.

'Remind me who he is again.'

'Dealer. Suspected to be running gangs. Slippery as an eel. He's been nicked several times for this and that, but we can never make it stick. There's always someone else who'll take the rap for him.'

'The type never to get his hands dirty if he can help it,' the Super said.

She was right. Parr employed other people for that. Was Lyall one of them, Casey wondered?

Only once had the combined efforts of the justice system managed to put Parr away, Casey reminded the Super. And even then it had been for a lesser charge, thanks to his brief, whom Casey was convinced had been as slippery as he was himself.

It must have been during his brief sojourn at Her Majesty's Pleasure that he'd either reconnected or taken up again with David Lyall aka Arlan Roberts, she suggested.

'The guy who disappeared?'

'Parr was spotted trying to intimidate Lyall outside Tony's where he worked as a volunteer. And the very next day he disappeared.'

'Interesting. Do they have history?'

'I've just this second found out they were both up at Lumbley together,' Casey said.

She'd discovered something else too. Lyall had taken a shine to his art teacher's name and pinched it for an alias.

'Why would he do that?'

'Maybe he admired Roberts. You know, the way he lived his life.'

She told the Super what she'd discovered about Arlan Roberts from the Surrey bobby. By all accounts he'd lived a good life, albeit one that had been prematurely curtailed. If Lyall had been determined finally to go straight, then who better to emulate than a man like Arlan Roberts?

'So this is what you were up to when you should have been at my meeting?'

Given that she didn't have a leg to stand on, Casey remained silent. The Super's expression was inscrutable. What punishment was she conjuring up in that head of hers, she wondered. She wished she'd just get it over with.

Finally, the Super spoke. 'I suppose it's all quite relevant,' she said. 'You need to find both of them. If Parr's back in Brockhaven it can only mean trouble. And if he's just recruited a sidekick then that's trouble times two.'

It looked as if Casey had got away with it.

★   ★   ★

Zach Daley lay on his unmade bed waiting for his cousin Kian to answer his call. He could have gone over to his house for this, but right now he was desperate to keep under the radar. All day at school he'd had to put up with people taking the mick. Just because of that fight in Starbucks the other day. He'd been there with the rest of his family and those Stocks scum. Course he had. But as soon as the cops turned up he'd slipped away. Given what he'd had in his pocket at the time, it had been a wise move.

Now the papers had got hold of it. He'd seen headlines on the placard outside the newsagent's. 'Feuding Families Stir It Up In Starbucks Skirmish', it said. At school, people knew better than to laugh in his face but he wasn't stupid. He knew they were talking about him behind his back.

At dinner time he'd gone to the chicken shop as usual. There were these lads from the Sixth Form hanging about in there, discussing what they were going to order. As soon as they clocked him he heard one call out to his mate who'd joined the queue, 'If you're getting coffee, mate, mine's a flatte.' Then the other one had turned round and said, 'OK, bruv, don't get in a froth.'

Course, they all burst out laughing then and he'd had no choice but to turn round and walk out without his food. Where did they get off, humiliating him like that? And in front of younger kids, too. Well, they'd be laughing on the other side of their faces sooner than they could imagine.

'Zach. What do you want?'

Finally, Kian had picked up. He sounded gruff. Like he wished he hadn't answered.

'Have you thought about what I said?' Zach said. 'About starting off on our own?'

There was a long silence at the other end. There was something so irritatingly wimpy about his cousin that made him want to shake him sometimes.

'Come on, bro. Think about it. You and me. While we both carry on working for them we'll never make any real money.'

'We make enough,' Kian said.

Kian was fourteen. He had no idea what real money there was to be made in this business.

'I recruited you, remember,' he went on. 'Don't you think you owe me?'

Another silence. Perhaps he should try

another tack. If Kian thought he was being threatened he might just walk away before Zach could explain his brilliant plan.

'If it weren't for us they'd be floundering right now,' he said, more cajoling this time. 'Think about it. Who is it who'll be taking the rap if they get caught? Not them. Because we don't even know their names. They've got our names though haven't they, Kian? Our names and the names of all the other runners.'

He waited for this to sink in. Kian finally spoke.

'Where would we get the stuff to start up on our own in the first place?' he said. 'And where would we sell it? Not round here.'

He wasn't saying no, at least.

'There's other places than Brockhaven,' Zach said. 'We wouldn't be in competition.'

'We wouldn't want to be,' Kian said. 'They'd kill us if they thought that was what we were doing.'

'Well, we just have to be smarter than them, that's all,' Zach said. 'We do what they do. Keep our hands clean. Put someone else in the frame. And I've got the very person.'

'Who?'

Finally, his cousin had woken up and smelled the coffee. It was about time too.

'You're gonna love this, bro,' he said. 'It's that little snake, Johnny Martin. If anyone needs teaching a lesson then it's him.'

★   ★   ★

Casey sat in the headmistress's study, facing her across her desk. The room was modern, light and airy, with a window looking out onto the playing field, where a game of football was underway. Sitting next to her was Giles, leaning forward, his elbows planted on his long skinny legs, spread wide. She couldn't see his face because of all that floppy hair. It was impossible to imagine what he must be thinking.

When she'd had the call from the school she'd dropped everything, jumped in the car and driven straight there.

'I'm sorry to have to say that Giles has been involved in a fight,' the school receptionist had said. 'As he's staying with you while his parents are out of the country, I'm going to have to ask you to come in.'

The headmistress was the homely type. She had a kind face, Casey thought. But Giles was oblivious to her smile and her gentle entreaties to tell her everything that had happened.

'I've spoken to the other boy,' she said. 'He says you punched him in the face. Is that true, Giles?'

If he were her son, Casey would touch him. Very likely she'd tell him to sit up straight and answer the question. But he was a stranger to her. She had no idea who she might be dealing with here. He'd been at the school two days and already he was in trouble. Was it a habit of his, going round punching people? Or was it some sort of protest against his current situation?

Since he'd arrived, all she'd been able to see was a quiet, polite boy who cleared his plate at meal times and picked up after himself uncomplainingly. But she'd been a police officer for long enough to know that what you saw was not always what you got.

What did he really think about being dumped in a house with strangers in a town he didn't know? Then thrown into a new school slap bang in the middle of his GCSE year? It was an awful lot for a young boy to cope with.

'Giles,' she said, quietly. 'It might help if you told us your version of what happened.'

Giles shifted in his seat, as if he were considering the idea. Then he gave a long sigh.

'We're here to listen, Giles,' the headmistress said.

She offered Casey an encouraging smile, as if she imagined Casey might somehow magic some words of explanation from the boy. Don't ask me, Casey felt like saying. I barely know him from the next boy in your school.

'He's right,' Giles said. 'I did punch him. So you might as well get it over with. My punishment I mean.'

The two women eyed each other cautiously.

'Do you have a reason?' they said simultaneously.

Giles shook his head. They tried again, but it was to no avail. Which was why, just ten minutes later, Casey was back in the car, this time with Giles in the passenger seat, heading home. One week's suspension, Casey mused, turning into the drive. How was she going to explain that to Giles's parents?

★ ★ ★

'You and me need to have a chat later,' Gran had said earlier, when she'd been putting his tea on the table. Usually they ate together, but Thursdays was her night for Pilates and she wouldn't miss that for anything.

Johnny hadn't asked what about because he thought he knew. There was something about the way she kept watching him from the corner of her eye, then as soon as he looked back she'd turn away. She'd left soon after, thank God, because he'd never have got away so easily otherwise.

He didn't need any more stress. Not after this morning. All day at school he'd been holding his breath, waiting to be sent for. He'd been terrified. But in the end Miss Buchan hadn't wanted to see him after all. If she'd believed Zach's words — that the new boy had punched him because he said Zach had given him a funny look — then it had to mean that that Giles or whatever he was called hadn't grassed Zach up.

But how much had he seen? And what had he heard? He'd definitely seen that Zach had had Johnny in a headlock. Had he heard Zach say he was going to keep him there till Johnny promised he'd do this drop tonight? Surely not or he'd have reported it.

'You back me up,' Zach had threatened, once he came out of Miss Buchan's room. 'Or you'll be in trouble.'

It hardly seemed fair that Zach had said he still owed him one, even though it was the new boy who'd been suspended, while Zach had been let off scot-free. But that's exactly what had happened. And there was no way he could get out of this now. He was expected round the back of some warehouse on the business estate in five minutes, where he was expected to hand over the drop to the usual dealer.

It was a funny place to meet, Johnny thought, as, once off the main road, he got off his bike. Down this narrow lane then take a right, Zach had said. And no bike lights. Just in case the rozzers are about. Johnny's heart was beating fast. He didn't like the dark at the best of times. But this was an unfamiliar place and it was dead dark. No street lights and no cars. But he knew the rozzers could easily be lying in wait for him. Any second now they could flood him with lights.

Keeping his head down, he plodded on. The lane had narrowed to a track now — all overgrown with weeds and stuff that kept brushing his legs as he tried to navigate his way through. His bike wheels kept getting stuck on the uneven ground.

And then he thought he heard something. The crack of a branch overhead. The crunch of dry earth behind him.

Someone breathing. He quickened his steps to match his breath. You're being soft, he told himself. Just a few more yards and he'd be out in the clearing.

The blow landed on him from out of nowhere, stunning him, throwing him forward so he lost his footing. Another blow and then another, bursting like petals in his head. Someone was speaking. Two different voices. They were looking for something, urging each other on to find it quickly. Their hands were rough. He felt their boots against his body as they moved round him. And then they were gone and it was just him and the cold hard ground beneath him.

★　★　★

Brockhaven was too small a place to stay hidden for long. Ever since Steve Parr had caught up with him that day at Tony's, David hadn't been able to stop looking over his shoulder. He'd been sleeping on Linda's sofa out Earlham Bridge way while he'd been working at Tony's. It hadn't been the best solution, but he'd been skint so what else could he have done?

He'd left the house without even saying goodbye and thanks for the hospitality, which was probably a bit ungrateful, considering what Linda had had to put up with. But he'd had no choice. He couldn't be found there. As soon as Parr realised he'd left Tony's, he'd know immediately that it was because he didn't want to have anything to do with him. And Parr wouldn't like that.

The man had contacts. Once he started looking for him properly somebody was bound to creep out of the woodwork and give him an address. Should he have said something to Linda? Warned her Parr might come sniffing round? She was on her own these days and there was a kid to think about too. What would Parr do to the place — to her — if he did go round and she told him she didn't know where he'd gone? The man was a psycho, no doubt about it.

If he'd have had the money for the bus he'd have left for London. He could lose himself in all those millions of people.

But London would finish him. It'd be the same story all over again — hustling just to stay alive. He'd done some bad things in his life and he didn't want to go back to his old ways.

That's why, in the end, he decided to stay local. He didn't know how long this casual work would last. It was back breaking and it paid crap money. But the job came with a bed and some half-decent food and it was far enough away from Steve Parr's manor to make him feel, if not safe, then less exposed at least.

He missed Tony's though. The staff, the people who came in. When he was there he'd felt he was doing something good. Becoming a better person.

David chucked another pile of bulbs in his bucket. He stood up for a moment to relieve his aching back. Eight hours sifting daffodil bulbs out of rows of rock hard mud. It was no more than slave labour, really, when you thought about it.

What would Arlan Roberts have done in his situation, he wondered, staring up at the bleak sky. Told Parr to get lost and find another lackey? Or that as far as he was concerned he'd done enough dirty work for him in the past and had no intentions of getting his hands dirty for him again?

It took a man of courage to talk like that. David might have taken Arlan's name, but he had none of his bravery. Facing death like that. He — David — was a coward. He knew that should Parr find him, then he might as well forget all those dreams of turning over a new leaf. He'd tried so many times over the years to shake him off.

When he landed at Lumbley Prison and started doing those art classes with Arlan, he felt freer than he'd ever done outside. Then who should turn up but Parr? Of all the cells in all the world. He was back to square one. He was always going to be back at square one as long as Steve Parr knew where he was. He would never pass 'go'.

His phone rang. Even before he answered it, he knew who it was. He felt suddenly sick. He fumbled in his pocket, pulled out the phone then dropped it. He picked it up, brushed off the dirt, then put it to his ear, without glancing at the number. He knew what it would say. Caller unknown. Parr wasn't stupid.

'You took your time.'

Congeniality and menace in the same voice. How was that possible?

'Steve. How did you get this number?'

'Never mind about that. I've got a little job for you,' Parr said. 'Coupla my lads down Brockhaven way. They're getting a bit too big for their boots. Need teaching a lesson. Know what I mean?'

David knew what was coming next.

'And I think you should be the one to let them have it.'

4

Dinner that evening had been a very taut affair. Giles, who seemed to have withdrawn completely into himself, kept his eyes fixed on his plate, ignoring all attempts to draw him into the conversation. By contrast Dom seemed compelled to fill the silence with a volley of empty chatter. It was all Casey could do not to tell him to put a sock in it. When Giles finally rose from the table, took his plate over to the dishwasher and declared he was going to his room, she gave an inward sigh of relief.

As soon as he'd left Casey pounced on Finlay. She knew it was unfair to put her son on the spot. But what else could she do if Giles refused to open up about the events that had led to his suspension? Sadly, it soon became apparent that she was wasting her time. Finlay was just as uncommunicative as Giles had been.

'Mum, I'm in Year Seven,' he said, in an

exasperated tone. 'Giles is a Year Eleven. We don't talk to them and they don't talk to us.'

He mopped up a puddle of ketchup with his last chip and popped it into his mouth. Casey had planned to cook lasagne from scratch tonight after Giles — in a rare moment of revelation — had declared how much he loved Italian food. But all thoughts of conjuring up anything more imaginative than oven chips and fish fingers had gone completely out of her head after that meeting with the head teacher. All she'd wanted was to get as far away from the school grounds as it was as possible to get.

Last night, round about half past ten, Giles had wandered into the kitchen for a glass of water, presumably hoping he could slip in and out without anyone spotting him. But he hadn't reckoned on Casey being there. She'd been sitting at the table, silently contemplating the contents of the biscuit tin and wishing she possessed the kind of willpower that made her want to choose a raw carrot over a chocolate digestive. He turned up just as she was going in for the biscuit. That's when she'd offered him one and he'd accepted and they'd made this small talk about their favourite food. It was a breakthrough, she'd thought. He was thawing out, beginning to feel at home.

But after today's events any closeness between them — real or imagined — had melted clean away. Right now she doubted that the distance between them could get any wider.

'But surely you must have heard something?' she demanded. 'I'd have thought it would have been all over the school within minutes!'

Finlay's expression was one of total bafflement.

'Mum,' he said. 'Swear down. First thing I knew about Giles getting suspended was this afternoon, when I got in.'

Boys, Casey couldn't help thinking, scornfully. No doubt he'd been too busy chasing Pokemon in his breaks to listen to any gossip. If he'd been a girl he'd have had the whole story by now.

'So you can't even tell me the name of the other person in the altercation?' she

65

said, aware she was pursuing this line of enquiry far longer than she probably ought.

'Leave it, Casey,' Dom muttered. 'Don't drag Finlay into this.'

He reminded her how late it was. Had this been an ordinary day Finlay would have been on his way to bed right now. Which was where they all should be, probably, he added.

'I just want to get to the truth, that's all,' Casey snapped, poo-pooing his suggestion about bed. 'Giles is holding something back and I would like to understand what. He's living in my house, remember.'

'You should ring his mum and dad,' Finlay suggested. 'He's their son, not yours. Let them deal with it.'

'It's not that simple, Fin.' Dom was on his feet now, determinedly clearing the rest of the table to signal that as far as he was concerned the discussion was over. But Finlay clearly disagreed.

'Well I don't see why Mum can't interrogate him the way she's interrogating me.' Turning to Casey, he said, 'It's not fair. Just because I'm your son it doesn't mean I'm going to do your dirty work for you!'

Casey drew in her breath, shocked at Finlay's reaction.

'Whoa!' Dom yelled from the sink. 'That's no way to speak to your mother.'

'It's okay,' Casey said. 'He's right. I shouldn't be involving him.'

'And anyway, even if I did know anything, I wouldn't tell you,' Finlay said. 'I'm no grass.'

Now it was Casey's turn to be angry. Where had he got that stupid idea from, she demanded, almost shaking with fury? Did he have any idea of the human misery perpetuated by criminals in every street on every estate in the UK all because of that stupid macho code of silence? Finlay mustn't ever be afraid to speak out for justice, she said. She hoped he understood that.

'Okay, okay,' he said. 'I get it.' He was holding out her phone, gazing at the screen. 'Your phone's been ringing for ages. Someone called Julie Martin.'

Casey snatched her mobile from her son's hand, glad of the interruption. She knew she could have handled this better but Finlay's ridiculous assertion that he'd never be a grass had infuriated her. No doubt there was more of this laddish talk to come as he grew older. Her influence on him was bound to decrease as the influence of his peers grew stronger. What if he ended up turning his back on the values he'd learned at home altogether? And what if, having Giles under his roof, some of the older boy's influence rubbed off on him? Perhaps he was even beginning to think of the boy as some kind of hero! It didn't bear thinking about.

Julie sounded distraught. At first Casey could make neither head nor tail of her words. She caught the name Johnny several times. She thought she heard the words 'Pilates' and 'dinner'. She told Julie to start again and slow down this time.

'It's Johnny,' she said, her breath coming in short gasps. 'I should have said something before. But I thought it would go away. It's nearly ten o'clock, Casey and he's not come home. I think he's out there, dealing drugs. And I'm frightened of what might happen to him.'

David had had his orders from Parr. I want you to shake them, he'd said. Show them runners who's boss. It had been easy enough to find them. Kids like that never strayed too far away from their ends. Out there in the big wide world they were just kids. But in their own neighbourhood they had status.

He'd been watching the two boys from the park bench for a while now. They'd got hold of some cans and were drinking from them, going from swing to round-about to slide and back again, laughing and pushing each other, while a small gang of youngers looked on. Kids who would have been home in bed now if they'd had mums and dads who cared about them.

Watching the two of them showing off was like stepping into his own past. One was bigger and older than the other. He had the swagger of someone who thought he was cock of the walk. His little mate deferred to him at all times, laughing when he laughed, drinking when he drank, continually glancing at him for approval and ultimately failing to win the admiration of the kids standing round. They only had eyes for the big man.

It could have been him and Parr fooling around in the park fifteen, sixteen years ago. Would the relationship between these two boys turn out the same, he wondered, slowly getting up from the bench and moving silently towards them? He sincerely hoped not, for the sake of the smaller one.

He'd thought about how he was going to handle this, right from the moment he'd found himself agreeing to do Parr's dirty work for him again. Parr would have the two of them shanked without batting an eyelid. If his information was correct then what they'd done was unforgiveable, he insisted. He'd be letting them off lightly with a knife wound.

Miraculously, David had managed to talk him down. Let me do it my way, he'd said. They're just kids. Remember what we were like at that age? Always trying to push the boundaries? They just need a good talking to, that's all. They'll be as good as gold after that. He'd brought up a few memories of former times, when Parr himself had shown a similar contempt for authority at their age. He'd even made him laugh about it. Shown him in a hero's light, which was something Parr always enjoyed.

He hated himself for doing it, of course. And for the way he'd allowed himself to slip right back into the role he'd been cast in as early as seven years old, when he'd first met Parr. But what choice did he have?

The only way to get Steve Parr out of his life for good would be to kill him. But he didn't have the guts to do that. In his life up to now he'd tasted violence more than once. He'd had plenty of time inside to come to the conclusion that he was never going to lay a finger on another human being that way again. And he was going to stick to his decision.

'What do you want, mister?'

It was the cocky one that spoke first. Arrogant little beggar. David took an instant dislike to him. Another five years and he'd either be running his own business or inside. The smaller, younger one was silent, staring up at David with sleepy, somewhat vacant eyes.

'You a paedo or something?' he went on.

Predictably, the smaller one sniggered at this remark. That was his role. To applaud his mate's witticisms. He used to be the same with Parr. David took a deep breath, willing himself to control his mounting irritation.

'I've got a message,' he said. 'I'm here to let you know we're onto you.'

The younger one immediately stopped laughing. He looked suddenly fearful. The older one tried to hide his own discomfort but David knew he'd made a hit. Perhaps smelling trouble, the gang of youngers had suddenly dispersed leaving the three of them alone.

'Who's we?' the older one ventured.

'I think you know.'

The boy shifted from foot to foot and fixed his eyes on the ground.

'I'm just the messenger,' David said. 'Next time it won't be me paying you a visit. It'll be someone you really need to be scared of. And it won't be just a word he'll be giving you either.'

The smaller boy looked terrified now. The older one was doing a rubbish impersonation of someone who wasn't. David turned round, slowly and deliberately, and began to walk away, feeling a weight off his shoulders. His work here was done and there'd been no violence.

But then the older one spoke again. 'Well, whoever it is you can tell him from me that I ain't frightened of him,' he said. 'And you can tell him too that he can . . .'

He didn't finish his sentence. The other boy grabbed him, pleading with him not to say anything more. Rage swelled up inside David. This kid was crazy. He had to be, to send a direct challenge to Parr like that. By rights he should lay him out right now. If only for his own good. Because Parr was going to want to know every detail of this exchange and it was no use him keeping anything back. Parr had always known how to get the truth out of him.

Walk away, he told himself. Don't look

back. That way if there was any trouble once he'd spoken to Parr, it couldn't be laid at his door. He made his way out of the park, stopping after a few yards to light a cigarette. Then he dialled Parr's number and told him everything that had passed. As soon as he'd put the phone down he regretted telling Parr how much the kid had disrespected him. Yes, he was an annoying little prankster. But he didn't deserve what was bound to be coming his way next.

Think before you speak, David. How many times had Arlan Roberts said those words to him back when he'd been banged up? These days he tried so hard to follow Arlan's advice. More often than not he succeeded. But at times like this, when he felt his back against the wall, that was when he forgot. And now that stupid kid was going to suffer for it.

'Mister?'

The little guy was there, half hidden behind a lamppost. He could only have been about twelve. What did he want?

'Have you got transport?' he said.

'I've got a car, yes,' he said, curious at

the question. 'But unless I get it back to its rightful owner before midnight it'll turn into a pumpkin.'

The boy looked at him as if he thought there could be some truth in this remark. David almost felt sorry for him. Anyone that gullible shouldn't have been dipping his toes in the murky waters of the drug world, however far removed from the centre he was.

'Why are you asking?'

The boy's eyes began to fill up with tears.

'I never wanted to do it in the first place,' he said, swiftly blinking them away. 'It was Zack who said we had to beat him up and take his drugs off him. I'm scared we might have killed him.'

David's heart skipped several beats. He hadn't got a clue what was going on here. He could just walk away. But someone somewhere was either dead or dying. He couldn't just turn his back on it.

'Car's just down this road,' he said. 'Follow me, kid.'

★   ★   ★

It had been no use Dom trying to remind Casey that she'd finished her shift for the day. She had no plans to go back to the station, she told him. But she needed to see Julie and that was an end to it.

'Just promise me you'll be back before midnight,' he'd said before she left.

It wasn't often Dom insisted on anything. But she could see he was serious. And to be fair, he had a point. They had enough on their plate with the two boys they were actually responsible for, without taking on a third. There were other detectives out there, Dom said. Not to mention the boys and girls out on patrol. If anyone could find Johnny and bring him home, then they could.

They were sitting in Julie's kitchen, on their second mug of tea. There had been no need for Casey to ask any questions. Julie had just talked and talked. About her initial suspicions that Johnny was going down the same road as his mum. And about the surliness, the secretiveness and the sudden outbursts when he thought she'd asked him too many questions. Not to mention the physical

76

evidence. The spoils of his trade, as she poetically described the new phone and the expensive trainers she'd found at the bottom of his wardrobe.

'Sometimes your heart keeps on ignoring the truth. No matter how many signals your head sends it,' Julie said.

She stared into the bottom of her empty mug. How stupid can one woman be, she added?

Casey put out a hand and patted Julie's. 'You're not stupid, Julie,' she said. 'Love can make us blind, that's all.'

She found herself telling Julie about Giles and how she'd never have guessed that he'd be the type to get himself suspended from school for beating up another boy. And about her recent conversation with Finlay and how impotent it had left her feeling.

'You think you know your own kids,' she said. 'But how many of us really do when it comes down to it?'

Julie glanced up from her mug and smiled, grateful for a glimpse of another woman's anguish.

'Do you think they'll find him Casey?

Alive and well, I mean?'

Casey fixed her with a keen gaze.

'You know I can't promise that, don't you, Julie?' she said 'Although I can promise we'll do our very best.'

It was just as she'd finished speaking that her phone rang. It was the Duty Sergeant.

'He's safe, Casey,' he said. 'Let his grandmother know he's at the General Hospital.'

'Thank God!' She breathed a sigh of relief. 'Is he okay?'

'They think so. A bit battered and bruised,' the Duty Sergeant said.

Casey immediately mouthed this information to Julie who put her hands over her face to hide her emotions.

'Can she come and see him?'

'Not tonight, the doctors said. Tell her to ring again in the morning.'

'I might have trouble holding her back,' Casey joked. 'Where did you find him?'

'We didn't. He was found outside by a porter. Propped up against a wall by a back entrance.'

'CCTV?'

78

'We're already onto it.'

'As soon as you get anything you wing the image over to my phone, right?' she demanded. 'I don't care how late it is.'

She'd promised Dom she wouldn't go into the station. But she'd said nothing about refusing to take calls.

When she got home the house was in darkness. All she wanted to do was climb the stairs and go to bed. But she was too tense and feared her tossing and turning would inevitably wake Dom. Perhaps a nightcap would put an end to her jitteriness.

Just as she was thinking this thought, she heard a noise. The sound of a door handle turning. The shuffle of feet. Where was that ruddy dog when you needed some protection, she mused, as she crept towards the kitchen, where she thought the sound had come from.

Giles stood in the open kitchen door. She saw him first, releasing the lead from Oscar's neck. As soon as the dog spotted her he gave a friendly bark and came padding towards her.

'Been for a midnight stroll have we?'

She bent down to pat him affection-
ately on the head, aware of Giles,
standing stiffly by his side. No doubt
already searching for excuses as to what
he'd been up to this time, when he should
have been tucked up in bed and fast
asleep.

★   ★   ★

Finding that other kid like that, limping
along the road in the pitch dark, had
scared the living daylights out of him.
When the kid had shrieked that that was
Johnny, he'd stopped the car and jumped
out to help him. Weaving all over the road
he'd been. Didn't seem to know where
he was or even who he was, so David
thought.

Course the kid had refused to get in
the car — who could blame him? He'd
already been beaten up once tonight!
There was nothing David could do but
get back behind the wheel and follow him
at a snail's pace till he finally gave up
trying to walk in a straight line and fell to
the ground.

He'd done the right thing, leaving him propped up against that back entrance. Someone would find him and get him to safety. All that was left for him to do now was get the car back to its rightful owner. He barely even knew the name of the guy he'd borrowed it from. Didn't think he even spoke English. But he'd helped him out in a tight corner and because of that, he didn't want to cross him. He needed all the friends he could get. Especially now, after what he'd done with his phone.

Sooner or later, the police would start asking little Johnny a few questions. They'd search his clothes, go through his pockets. And then they'd find David's phone and all those incriminating messages. He'd end up in prison again. Accessory after the fact. But he didn't care. Because this time he'd be taking Steve Parr down with him

5

'I couldn't sleep. So I thought I'd take Oscar for a walk.'

Giles stood in the middle of the kitchen, holding Oscar's lead with both hands and twisting it awkwardly as he spoke.

'I'm sorry for being such a nuisance,' he added.

'Don't be silly. You're not a nuisance. You didn't ask to come and stay here,' replied Casey.

His shoulders, which had been up round his ears when he'd first realised he'd been discovered creeping in the back way, relaxed. Finally, he met her gaze.

'How about you sit down and I'll make us a hot chocolate drink?'

Casey filled the kettle then reached inside the cupboard for the box of sachets. When she turned round Giles was already at the table, Oscar at his feet.

'You've made a good friend there,' she

said, emptying the powder into two mugs.

'I always wanted a dog,' he said, his head bowed so she couldn't see his face. 'But Mum and Dad think a dog would tie them down.'

Casey poured the water into the mug and stirred vigorously before taking them over to the table, setting them down and taking a seat opposite him.

'Too busy saving the world.'

There was no mistaking the bitterness in his voice. He raised the mug to his lips and blew on it.

'Thanks for this, by the way,' he added.

'I wish you'd tell me what happened at school, Giles,' she said. 'I don't know you very well. But, punching someone in the face. Well, it really doesn't seem your style.'

There was a tin of biscuits in the middle of the table. As soon as Casey removed the lid, Oscar sat up and looked interested.

'Besides, Oscar knows a wrong 'un when he meets one.' She tipped the tin towards him. 'I've seen the way he follows you about. That dog's the best judge of character of anyone I know.'

Giles smiled. It was a revelation. He was a very handsome boy. He selected a biscuit and slowly munched his way through it, deliberating whether or not he trusted Casey well enough to reply.

'My Dad's dead set against violence,' he said, finally. 'He always told me to walk away whenever there was trouble.'

'It's good advice.'

'But sometimes you can't do that. Not if you see someone getting hurt. You have to step in.'

'So who was getting hurt?'

He shrugged. 'Some kid. I don't know his name. I'd already stepped in before. He told me to butt out that time so I did. But I felt bad about it.'

His fingers wandered back to the biscuit tin. He glanced up at Casey for permission. She gave a nod.

'I could see he wasn't happy. This other kid was putting him under pressure. Following him about and forever getting in his face.'

'A bully,' Casey said.

Giles nodded. 'I should have told a

member of staff,' he said. 'But I had no real evidence other than what my instinct was telling me.'

He'd thought and thought about what he'd done, he said and the truth was that hitting that boy had been little to do with sticking up for the boy being bullied. It was more to do with his own ego.

'I just hated the thought of someone I had absolutely no respect for besting me,' he said. 'The Head was right to exclude me. I let myself down.'

'Not many boys your age are so self-aware, Giles,' Casey said, with a smile.

He made an embarrassed face.

'Right.' She glanced at the cooker clock. 'Finish that drink. It's late. You might not have school in the morning but I have a job to go to.'

Tomorrow meant a trip to the hospital to find out from Johnny who had put him there. If she could find the time, there was something else she'd like to do. That head teacher seemed like a reasonable human being. Probably had kids herself. With a bit of gentle persuasion, maybe

Casey could get her to take Giles back sooner than she'd originally decreed.

⋆   ⋆   ⋆

'What's going to happen to him, Casey?'

Julie hadn't let go of Johnny's hand all the time Casey had been by the boy's bedside. She held onto it in a gesture of defiance. If the police were coming for her grandson, then they were damn well going to have to take her with him.

Johnny, pale and with dark shadows under his eyes, lay back on his pillow with his eyes closed, clearly exhausted. Not just by yesterday's events, but by having to reveal everything that had led up to them in the previous months and weeks.

'It's not up to the police to decide these things,' Casey said, gently. 'He's confessed to carrying illegal substances to person or persons unknown, but he's not the dealer. And we haven't found any drugs on him. It's hard to know what we could charge him with, let alone how we could make a case for prosecution.'

'He's given names though, remember.

Those two boys from his school. That's bound to help his case.'

Casey agreed it would.

'It's them who should be locked up, not him,' Julie grumbled. 'They set him up.'

'And we'll get them, Julie. There's absolutely no need for you to worry about that.'

Johnny had been reluctant to talk at first. He didn't have a clue who it was who'd followed him all the way to the Business Park and jumped him just as he'd turned down that narrow lane, he said. But Casey wasn't sure if she believed him.

She thought back to the conversation she'd had with Finlay a couple of days ago. Even if I knew anything, he'd said, I'd never grass. Things being what they were, Johnny was bound to be of the same point of view. Poor boy would be terrified about what would happen to him if gave the names of his attackers.

Had he been older and they'd been alone, she would have pushed him. But he was just a kid and obviously still

87

traumatised. She had no desire to add to his trauma. In the end, it was Julie who'd persuaded him to give up the boys' names. If he had even the slightest inkling of who they might be, she said, speaking to him more sternly than Casey would have done herself, then he needed to tell the inspector. Otherwise it would be him in prison, while those two got off scot free.

Casey could have reminded Julie that Johnny was too young to go inside. But she wanted answers. And Johnny, albeit reluctantly, finally gave them to her. They were neither of them very bright, those boys who had attacked him, she figured. Zach and Kian Daley were the names he gave. She should have known that family would have a stake in this.

By all accounts, it had been a 'Don't tell him, Pike!' moment, with one of the boys calling out the other's name and suggesting the two of them should grab what they'd come for and get away. Johnny had felt someone pulling at his clothes and going through his pockets and through half-opened eyes he'd glimpsed Zach. Kian had been staring down at him anxiously, he said. Rather as if he wasn't blaming him as much as he blamed Zach. After that everything had been a blur, he said.

Casey's phone bleeped a message. She hoped it would be the head teacher. Before she'd done anything that morning, she'd rung the school, hoping to have a word with her about Giles's punishment and the possibility of curtailing it. All she'd got was the school secretary so she'd left a message asking the head to call back.

It wasn't the head but a picture file from the team who'd been examining the CCTV outside the hospital. Eager to see what it contained, Casey opened it. Immediately she knew who she was looking at.

'Johnny,' she said, quietly. 'I know you said earlier you don't remember how you got here.'

'I'm telling you the truth,' he said. 'I remember waking up in the dark then trying to find my way back to my bike. After that . . . '

'He's told you everything he remembers, Casey,' Julie butted in.

'I know, I know,' Casey said.

She held the phone out for Julie to look at. 'But look at that video, Julie.'

Julie squinted to get a better look. 'It's a bit blurred. Looks like someone getting out of a car.'

'That's right. See how he struggles to get Johnny out?'

'Oh,' Johnny said. 'Now I remember. There *was* a car. I think that's when I fainted.'

'Nice one, Johnny.'

Casey clicked on another file. This time it was a still close up.

'Now look at this,' she said. 'Recognise this guy, Julie?'

Julie stared at the picture. 'My God!' she said, as the penny dropped.

'David Lyall,' said Casey. 'Or as you know him, Arlan Roberts.'

'What's he got to do with all this?' Julie said.

'That's what we need to find out.'

Her phone was ringing. The name of the school popped up on her screen. Damn, this was hardly the moment to take a personal call. But if she missed it she'd end up playing cat and mouse with the head for the rest of the day.

'Excuse me for a second, will you?' she said, jumping up and heading for the exit.

The head teacher's manner seemed very different from the understanding one she'd adopted at their last meeting. When Casey explained why she wanted to speak to her, her response was a frosty one.

'You want Giles to come back to school tomorrow?' the head said, curtly. 'I think you know that under the circumstances that won't be possible.'

'What do you mean?' Casey was flabbergasted.

'You're a police inspector, aren't you?' she replied. 'I'd have thought you'd already have been informed. Giles has been arrested for assault. This time he's put Zach Daley in a coma.'

★ ★ ★

All she'd learned from the head teacher was that when Zach Daley hadn't turned up for school that morning and no one had rung in to say why, his class teacher had informed the office, who in turn had rung his home.

That's when they'd learned that Zach had been badly beaten up some time the previous night and was currently in intensive care. Naturally concerned, the head had phoned the police and informed them about the incident at school. Presumably one of Casey's colleagues, in their wisdom, had brought poor Giles in for questioning. Now it was up to her to sort it out.

She hadn't managed to get hold of the Super. But once in her car she got hold first of Dom, telling him to make sure Giles knew that he'd be out in no time and not to worry. And secondly, Gail, to tell her to allow no one to come near Giles till she got back to the station and spoke to him herself first.

At the station, Gail was standing guard outside the room where Giles, accompanied by his appropriate adult, Dom, had been taken.

'What's going on, Casey?' she said. 'Why has Giles been brought in?'

'It's a stupid mistake,' Casey said.

Bringing her up to speed with events as

speedily as possible, she informed her that it was Zack Daley who'd put Johnny Martin in hospital and that if anyone had come after Zack then it would have been for one reason — that he'd been caught with his fingers in the till.

If the headmistress was blaming Giles for beating Zack to a pulp, then she needed her head examined. He might have previously landed a blow on the boy but it had been a glancing one. Giles had taken full responsibility for it and was thoroughly mortified, she added.

'So who do you think is responsible?' Gail said. 'Zach Daley's clearly in no fit state to tell us. God knows when he will be either.'

'If we knew who was running those boys then we'd have our answer. Maybe David Lyall knows more than he's letting on.'

'How's he involved in all this?'

'He brought Johnny into hospital. I don't know if that makes him a saint or a sinner. But we need to find out.'

'I'll put out a call for Patrol to keep an eye out for him,' Gail said. 'We'll get our man, Casey.'

Casey's phone rang. It was Julie.

'You need to listen to this,' Julie said, dispensing with the usual greeting.

'What's happened?'

'Johnny's home now,' Julie said. 'But just as we were leaving, the nurse on duty stopped us. Said Johnny had left his phone behind. Johnny was in the loo so I took it from her.'

It didn't worry her that she didn't recognise it. She'd seen a phone at the bottom of Johnny's wardrobe a week ago and as far as phones went they all looked the same to her.

'Except Johnny swore it wasn't his,' she went on. 'So he scrolled down the numbers and, guess what?'

She sounded excited. 'Tell me,' Casey said.

'My number's on the list of contacts. And so is the number of Tony's. I think it's Arlan's phone.' She quickly corrected herself. 'Sorry, I mean David Lyall's.'

They had a lead. With a bit of luck, somewhere in that list of contacts was the number of whomever it was David Lyall was working with. She needed to get hold

94

of that phone as soon as possible.

'I'm coming round, Julie. Now.'

But then she remembered Giles. Right now, he'd be sweating in that cramped little waiting room, out of his mind with worry. Briefly, she explained his situation. Julie was shocked and wanted to know more but Casey was impatient to get on. She needed five minutes to reassure Giles, then she'd be on her way, she said.

'Meanwhile,' she said. 'Whatever you do, don't let that phone out of your sight.'

* * *

David stood outside Julie's house, plucking up the courage to knock on her door. He felt bad for lying to her, giving her a false name and a whole made-up history. She'd been so nice to him. Made him feel trustworthy and responsible. He longed to be that person again.

But with his luck, he doubted he'd ever get the chance. What with making sure the CCTV camera got a good look at him, then slipping his mobile into that kid's pocket before driving away, he'd done everything he could to make sure he'd be found, short of presenting himself at the police station with 'GUILTY AS CHARGED' stamped across his forehead.

This morning he'd got the sack for sleeping in and turning up for work two hours late. Now, he had no job and no roof over his head. He should have felt suicidal. But instead he felt weirdly relaxed. Like a man who'd been given just a few weeks to live and knew there was no point fighting it any more. Was that how Arlan Roberts had felt, when he'd been handed out his death sentence?

He'd done a sketch of Arlan, just before Arlan stopped coming in to teach them, once a week on Tuesday afternoons. He'd been proud of it. Everyone said how much like him it was. He'd been looking forward to showing it to him. But when it was time for the next lesson, Arlan didn't show up.

He didn't come the following week either. Nor the week after that, or the week after that. But David was still hopeful he'd come back and he could show him his sketch. He ignored the rumours at first. Arlan Roberts couldn't be dead. He didn't do drugs, didn't smoke or even drink much. He was a vegan, so he'd told David. Wasn't that supposed to be the healthy option? But it was true in the end. He'd got fed up of not knowing and had finally asked one of the screws, who confirmed it.

He'd never get to show him that sketch now. Nor would he get to tell him how grateful he was for teaching him to draw and for giving him back some self-respect. But he still had the chance to say those things to Julie.

Taking his courage in his hands, he rapped hard on the door. He almost bottled it and bolted back down the path. But it was too late. Someone was already coming to answer the door. When it opened it revealed a woman he'd never seen before. Tall. Sort of professional-looking. It wasn't Julie.

The first glance she gave him was one of irritation. Obviously he'd interrupted something. But then her brow unknotted. She was looking at him long and hard, like she thought she might know him from somewhere. Finally, her face cleared and her mouth relaxed into a welcoming smile.

'Well, who'd have thought it?' she said, opening the door wide for him to enter. 'The mountain has come to Mohammed. Come in, David. You're very welcome.'

★　★　★

They were waiting for a Skype call. It was like a family portrait. All of them grouped round the table — Finlay, Casey, Dom and Giles, centre stage. Even Oscar was determined to get a look in, nosing his way round each one of them, hoping for a leg up.

If this worked, it would be a miracle. It was the middle of the night in the unpronounceable village where Giles's parents were staying and electricity, let alone Wifi, was at a premium. Casey crossed her fingers for Giles. He must be desperate to speak to his mum and dad after all this time away from them.

It had been four weeks now. In that

time, thanks to David Lyall, Steve Parr had been arrested and charged with possessing class A drugs with the intention of dealing, thanks to a raid on his flat, which had been rammed to the four corners with drugs of every description.

Julie had been devastated at the thought of having to tell Johnny that his dad would be going to gaol for a long time. But Johnny took it very well. After all, he had his Gran, who loved him and had given him all the security he needed to cope with any amount of adversity life could throw at him.

No charges had been brought against him. Nor were any brought against David. Julie had spoken to the priest at the church and between them they'd offered him a full time job at Tony's. There was even a room to go with it. Last time Casey had seen him he'd told her — his face shining — that he'd signed up for evening classes in drawing. She had high hopes for that young man.

Giles had gone back to school the very next day, after he'd been allowed home with an apology from none other than the Super herself. He'd made friends and was doing well in his studies. There was talk of a girl. Not from him of course. But Finlay had seen him on several occasions deep in conversation with a petite blonde girl. A looker, so he said.

The computer made the weird bleeping sound it did to signal that Skype was working. Everyone sat up. The idea was that they'd all say hi then melt away so that Giles could have some precious time alone with his mum and dad.

The picture was a bit fuzzy. But there they were, Liz and Chris, both with eager, smiling faces, waving furiously. They all waved back, apart from Oscar, who barked a greeting instead. Chris was the first to speak.

'Hey Giles! What's been happening?' he said.

'Nothing much,' Giles replied.

Casey caught Dom's eye. He winked at her and she rolled her eyes. Boys! They'd always be a mystery to her.

The Other Diana

1

She must have agreed to this thing at Finlay's school. Not least because Finlay had thrust the proof under her nose when she'd questioned it. There, undeniably, squatting on the consent form Finlay had brought home, was her signature. A black, spidery scrawl that said 'Casey Clunes'.

At some point in the dim and distant past — probably when she'd been in such a hurry to get to work she'd have signed her own death warrant — Casey had agreed to speak to her son's class about what it was like to be a detective inspector with the Brockhaven Constabulary. And now that day had finally dawned.

Thirty pairs of eyes gazed up at her expectantly, perfectly quiet and perfectly still. All apart from Finlay, who shifted awkwardly in his seat and refused to look at her. Once upon a time, he'd have met her at the door, proudly announcing that here was his mummy come to tell them all about catching the bad men and locking them up.

But times had changed. That thing had happened whereby one night he'd gone up to bed with a cheery wave and a smile and next morning had come down with a new vocabulary of snarls and grunts and one-syllable words. He'd become a teenager and she, his mother, was an embarrassment.

'It wasn't my idea,' he'd scowled, when Casey initially denied all knowledge of the event. 'I should have kept my mouth shut when Miss Moody asked us if our mums had interesting jobs.'

Miss Moody was sitting next to her now, the two of them barricaded behind the form teacher's desk, in what felt to Casey like the direct line of fire of the class of thirteen-year-olds. With a name like Moody, Casey had conjured up a sour-faced, ill-tempered old witch, counting the months to her retirement. It had been a pleasant surprise to discover that she was in fact a woman in her thirties, pretty and smiley.

She reminded Casey of someone she'd met before. There was something about the eyes and the slope of the mouth. The name too — Rowan — struck a cord. She told herself she was being ridiculous. Wasn't there a webpage that contained pictures of every member of staff with their names attached? She must have looked at it some time, if only for a minute or two and with her memory for faces, this one, as Finlay's teacher, must have stuck. And yet . . .

'So, who has a question for Detective Inspector Clunes?' Miss Moody's question broke into her thoughts.

She willed Finlay to help her out since nobody seemed to want to be the first. But he seemed more interested in sliding as far down into his seat as possible. Any second now and he'd disappear completely. Finally, a round-faced, confident-looking girl with squat chestnut plaits raised her hand.

'What qualifications do you need to join the police?' the girl, who identified herself as Gemma, asked.

Casey made a mental note to keep her eye out for this young lady a few years down the line.

'Would you like to join the police, Gemma?' she asked, once she'd explained as briefly as possible the various routes an individual could take to gain admittance to the police service.

'Me? Oh, no,' Gemma said. 'I want to take over my dad's business. He sells cars. I reckon I'd make far more money doing that than being a cop.'

There was massive giggling and some eye-rolling at this. The boy sitting next to Gemma gave her a shove with his elbow.

'What?' she said, turning her aggrieved face towards him. 'She asked, didn't she?'

'Settle down, everyone,' Miss Moody said with a frown. 'And let's have some more questions.'

In the end, Casey had cause to be grateful for Gemma, despite her lack of diplomacy. Now she'd got the ball rolling, the questions began to flow thick and fast. How many murderers had she caught? Who was her favourite TV detective? What was the worst thing she'd seen? (She had to dodge that one.)

Casey began to relax. Even Finlay re-emerged from beneath his desk and appeared to start taking an interest. All too soon, her allotted forty minutes were up.

'There's just time for one more question,' Miss Moody said.

Casey had noticed a girl in a hijab with beautiful eyes who'd been waggling her hand for a long time.

'Go ahead,' she said, with a nod of her head in the girl's direction.

'You said you started off as a police constable,' the girl, who gave her name as Aicha, said.

'That's right,' Casey said.

'So what did you have to do to get promoted to detective constable?'

'Well, that's an interesting question and I'm glad you raised it,' Casey replied. 'I think we have the TV police dramas to thank for portraying plain-clothed officers as superior in rank to uniformed ones.'

She explained that in fact that there was no difference in rank between the two. The difference was simply in their roles. Uniformed officers were generally first at the scene of a crime and were more forensically aware, she explained. They also made the arrest as a rule, whereas detectives were more involved in the interview process. She'd had to attend courses to learn how to question a suspect and to get a more extensive knowledge of the law, she said. But if she wanted to she could ask to be transferred to uniform any time she liked.

Right on cue, the bell rang. Casey's ordeal was over. Except in the end it had turned out to be no ordeal at all. If only she could stay here all morning. That way she could avoid that tricky meeting with the Super.

★　★　★

They were in the staff room, where Casey had been invited to join Miss Moody for morning coffee. The teacher had led her over towards a battered old sofa where Casey now sat, taking in the hustle and bustle of the busy staff room and waiting for her return with a much needed drink.

It was from there she noticed someone on the other side of the room scrutinising her. As soon as the woman caught

Casey's eye she beamed at her as if they were the oldest of friends and came bustling over to join her on the settee.

'Jilly Seddon, Head of English,' the woman said, extending a limp, veined hand. 'You must be Finlay's mother.'

'Oh, dear. What's he done now?' said Casey, only half-joking.

The woman threw back her head and chuckled, revealing a great deal of gum and a set of long and rather yellowish teeth. The black suit she wore, with a peek of white at the neck, drained her complexion of any brightness. Her lips were painted a deep blood red and the way the colour bled at the edges of her mouth added to the vampire effect. It was hard to put an age to her but her formal and ultra-polite way of expressing herself rather suggested to Casey that she'd never see sixty again.

'Oh you have no cause to worry, Mrs Talbot,' the woman said.

Casey didn't correct her. Talbot was Dom's name. It had been much easier, when Finlay was born, to give him his father's name rather than go down the double-barrelled route.

'It's just, I heard from Rowan that you'd be coming in today, and wanted to take the opportunity to have a chinwag,' she said. 'In fact, Finlay has a great talent for writing stories.'

A sudden rush of motherly pride quashed Casey's previous suspicions that Finlay was in Big Trouble.

'Oh well, it's his dad he takes after in that department,' she said. 'Not me.'

Dom was a journalist by profession, though since the Brockhaven Gazette — where he'd worked for years — had amalgamated with two other small local newspapers, his writing career had diverged down several other directions.

'Well whoever he gets it from, his last story was brilliant,' the teacher said, 'the title I gave them all to write was 'A Busy Place'. Finlay set his story inside his head.'

Such an imaginative interpretation, she added, beaming. But then her expression changed.

'The thing is, however, Mrs Talbot,' she said, leaning in closer. 'I'm not sure how the examination board would react to his somewhat quirky interpretation of the title.'

'How do you mean?'

'Well, they might think he wasn't answering the question,' she said. 'They might fail him.'

Casey heard a chink of mugs. Miss Moody was back. Sally Seddon greeted her colleague with a frosty smile which was more than matched by Miss Moody's own glacial greeting.

'Do you mind if I take this seat, Sally?' she said. 'Only I have some paper work to go through with my visitor.'

Sally Seddon leapt to her feet nimbly. She was very spry, Casey mused. Clearly, here was a woman who refused to allow age to get the better of her.

'Of course, my dear,' she said, extending her hand once more. 'So lovely to meet you, my dear.'

'I guess this was about Finlay having too much imagination,' Miss Moody said as the two of them watched Sally Seddon's retreat to the far corner of the room where she pounced on some other poor unsuspecting staff member. 'She wanted me to penalise him because she said he needed to learn to write for the exam before he reached Year Ten.'

'Seriously?'

According to Sally Seddon, Finlay had too much imagination, she added.

'However can a child have too much imagination?' said Miss Moody. 'This damn education system is making little robots of the next generation.'

She was clearly exasperated at the thought.

'So, did you mark him down?' Casey wanted to know.

If she had, then Finlay hadn't mentioned it. Miss Moody shook her head. On the contrary, she said, she'd given him full marks and a merit. She grinned a wide mischievous grin. It made her look about sixteen. And it was then that Casey remembered where she'd met her before.

'I think I know you,' she said. 'In fact, I'm sure I've been inside your house.'

'Oh?' The teacher's expression changed. It was as if she was hiding something.

'It was years ago. I was still in uniform. You'd been ill. I think you were in bed.'

The years suddenly fell away. She was standing in the doorway. Rowan Moody, under her duvet, was almost hidden by her mother's enveloping arms. What she could see of her face was a streak of tears and a mass of hair. Casey didn't want to be there. But she was a woman. And women were good at this sort of thing, so the rest of the team insisted. Something to do with her 'feminine touch'. They were all men, of course.

'You must have been the police officer who came to interview me about Diana.' Miss Moody's voice trembled.

Diana Hunter had been sixteen years of age when her body had been washed up along a stretch of beach called Keepers' Cove. The case had never left Casey. Not just because a young girl had died who would never live to realise her potential. But because of the wrongful arrest that had speedily followed and the hurt that had caused the family.

There was another reason too, that made it impossible for anyone local to forget the day Diana Hunter's body was washed ashore. Her death coincided with the death of someone whose celebrity vastly overshadowed this much more local tragedy.

'Diana was my best friend,' Miss Moody said. 'Though in the months leading up to her death we'd sort of fallen out.'

They'd both been classmates here at St Bede's, she added.

'Of course, she was a pupil here,' Casey said. 'I should have remembered.'

'The school doesn't advertise it. As I'm sure you can imagine.'

The bell went for the end of break. The teacher drained her mug.

'Hey ho,' she said. 'Back to the coal face.'

They both rose to their feet whereupon Miss Moody volunteered to walk Casey to the exit.

Outside the staffroom the corridor teemed with children of all sizes heading towards their next class. The two women dodged the throng and the intoxicating mist of over-sweet perfume, Lynx and socks and finally made it through the scrum to reception.

'Well, thanks for today, Miss Moody,' said Casey.

'Please, you must call me Rowan,' the teacher replied. 'Miss Moody makes me feel so ancient.'

'And you must call me Casey,' Casey replied. 'Detective Inspector sounds far too formal.'

'Then it's a deal.'

The two women shook hands on it.

'I hope I haven't upset you. Bringing Diana's death up after all this time,' Casey said.

Rowan shook her head. It was a long time ago, she said. Time had moved on.

Casey liked this young woman. She'd seen how she interacted with the children and how fond and respectful of her they all seemed. Besides, how could anyone dislike a teacher who maintained that too much imagination in a child was simply not possible?

She'd recognised the look that had passed between Rowan and Sally Seddon back in the staffroom, too. Once upon a time she'd been there herself, taking orders from those in a superior position for whom she'd held little respect. It was toxic and debilitating and she'd hate for Rowan to lose the enthusiasm for her subject and the love for her pupils that she clearly possessed.

It was tempting to say something — to offer some advice. Don't stay where you're not appreciated. Get out and find a school where the person who leads the team thinks the same way as you. Better still, go for the top job yourself.

But it was far better for Rowan to reach a decision about where she wanted her career to go herself. In the exact same way Casey herself had done, in fact, all those years ago, when she'd grown tired of the limits her job as a PC had put upon her.

* * *

Superintendent Jess Morgan was a fair woman and Casey had a huge amount of respect for her — very possibly because she knew the feeling was mutual. But times were desperate and money was tight. Frankly there weren't enough bodies to go round.

Which was why Casey had been roped in to take over as strategic lead on the Hate Crime Incident Committee when Jayne Mitchell had gone off on maternity leave six months previously.

Now, however, it transpired that Jayne wasn't coming back, having made the decision that she preferred motherhood to police work. So Casey's temporary position had become permanent. As if she didn't have enough to do, which was exactly what she'd told Jess in their meeting.

'That was where you made your big mistake, my friend.'

Once out of the meeting Casey had done what she always did when she needed either a shoulder to cry on or someone to vent her frustrations on. She sought out her best friend, Sergeant Gail Carter and dragged her off to the canteen for a coffee.

'What do you mean?'

Gail gave an exaggerated sigh.

'Because if you'd not said that, then she'd have had no opportunity to remind you you'd just been out on a jolly all morning talking to a bunch of kids at St Bede's,' she said.

'Fair point,' Casey conceded.

'Don't look so miserable. It's not so bad. How many of those committee meetings are there in a year? Six at the most, surely?'

'I guess. But you know me and committees. All that 'point of order' stuff. It's just not for me.'

Gail gave her a sympathetic look.

'Well, maybe she'll change her mind,' Gail said. 'It has been known.'

Casey snorted. 'No chance,' she said. 'She actually told me it'd take at least a murder to get me out of it.'

'That sounds a bit heartless. Even for her,' Gail said. 'Anyway, enough of all that. You've still not told me everything about this morning.'

Casey quickly cheered up once she'd got into her stride. Gail chuckled when Casey related the Gemma incident and sympathised when she described Finlay's initial disdain.

'But the most interesting thing was that the teacher, Rowan Moody, knew Diana

Hunter,' Casey said. 'In fact they were best friends.'

'Diana who?' Gail threw her a quizzical look.

'Of course, you weren't here then. It was back in '97. I was a lowly police constable. The only woman, bar two, in the entire investigation team.'

'What happened to her?'

Diana Hunter went missing at the start of the school holidays, Casey explained. Casey was roped in to do door-to-door enquiries alongside several other officers.

'I lost count of how many doors I knocked on,' Casey said. 'And how many statements I took. But during those two weeks we were looking for her, we got nowhere.'

And then, she added, on August 31st, a Sunday morning, Diana's body was discovered. It looked like she'd drowned. Gail sat forward in her chair.

'Seriously?' she said. 'August 31st 1997? You're joking!'

Casey shook her head. 'No, I'm not. Same day. Same name.'

It was weird, she said, how the town had reacted.

'It was almost like they'd got the two Dianas mixed up in their heads. Flowers began to appear at the cenotaph in the market square. Someone even started a condolence book.'

It was a crazy time, she added.

'You said it looked like she'd drowned.' Gail traced quotation marks in the air around the words 'looked like'.

'Till forensics revealed she was already dead before she reached the water. Which rather suggested someone else had had a hand in it.'

'Did they get anyone for it?'

Casey sighed. 'Oh yes,' she said. 'Very conveniently, they arrested some 18-year-old kid with learning difficulties.'

'But you don't think he did it?'

'At the time I was sure he hadn't. He was being bullied, in my opinion. I tried to argue his case with the rest of the team. But they'd already decided it was him. All lads together and me the only woman, you know what it was like back then.'

'Tell me about it,' Gail said. 'Sounds like you're saying they were responsible for the bullying.'

'Some of it. Or at least they preferred to believe the mob rather than the evidence.' Casey had been studying her hands. She looked up and met Gail's eyes. 'Anyway, they took me off the case then. Sent me to guard the flowers at the cenotaph.'

And that's when she'd decided to apply for the CID.

'Is he still inside?' Gail said.

'Good God, no. The CPS threw the case out through lack of evidence. It's still an open case, though it's been scaled down to zero since. And there it will remain till someone comes forward with some compelling evidence.'

'Is that your phone ringing, Casey?'

Casey had been so wrapped up in her story that she hadn't heard it. When she glanced at the phone screen she recognised the number as being St Bede's. Her stomach plummeted. An accident, she thought. Finlay. But thankfully it wasn't. It was Rowan Moody.

'Finlay gave me your number, I hope you don't mind,' she said. Her words were hesitant, her tone strained. 'But I

121

think I need to talk to you.'

'Go ahead,' said Casey.

There was a long pause before Rowan spoke again. 'This morning,' she said. 'It was when you brought up Diana.'

There was another long pause.

'Go on,' Casey said, encouragingly.

'I started thinking about her again,' she went on. 'That last time I spoke to her on the phone.'

Another pause. Casey wasn't going to ruin things by filling it.

'And I keep wondering. What if what she said to me the day before she went missing had something to do with how she died?'

2

Rowan didn't want to talk to her right now. Frankly, if she never spoke to Diana Hunter again it would be too soon. She was supposed to be her best friend. But what sort of best friend couldn't be bothered to pay you a visit all those weeks you were in hospital or pick up the phone to find out how you were once you were home?

She'd not even sent a get well card. Unless you counted the class one. Diana had squeezed her signature sideways into the only available space, somewhere between Aileen Wright and Chesney Brookes, with three scrawled kisses attached. It was obvious to Rowan it had been a last minute thing someone had had to remind her about.

'Rowan! Are you coming down? Diana's waiting on the phone.'

There'd be no peace till she went downstairs and took that call. Rowan eased herself up from the bed and swivelled her feet round till they met the floor. No dizziness. So far, so good. She felt a bit stiff, though. And cold, even though the sun was blazing outside. She was tempted to wrap herself up in the big woolly jumper hanging on the peg behind the door.

But Mum would see and draw her own conclusions and she'd start nagging her with questions about how she was feeling. So she gritted her teeth and decided to go without, crossing her bare arms against her chest to ward off the chill probably nobody else could feel as she headed downstairs.

Once there, Rowan took the receiver from Mum. She waited till she could make sure her mother was out of sight and fully out of earshot before she spoke. It was important to sound languid, like she wasn't bothered about getting this call one way or the other.

'Di. Well, this is nice,' she said. Then, unable to keep the spite out of her voice, she added, 'I'm surprised you could spare the time.'

'Don't start,' Diana snapped. 'I'm talking to you now, all right?'

The trouble with Diana was that when it came to spite she could always go one better. Rowan sometimes wondered if that was the reason she'd made friends with her all those years ago at Primary School on their first morning. It was far better to be Diana's friend than her enemy.

'So what have you been up to then, while I've been lying on my sick bed?'

Diana wasn't even going to bother asking how Rowan was, she was certain of that. There was a long pause on the other end of the line, then a dramatic sigh. She guessed Diana was scratching around for an excuse.

'I would have come and seen you, you know,' she said at last. 'But the hospital said only two people round the bed at any one time. I couldn't get past your Mum and Dad. They were always there.'

She had a point.

'Although I've been home a fortnight

now,' Rowan reminded her.

'Yeah and I've been at school. Remember that place?'

Rowan had missed most of the last term because of this stupid illness of hers. Which meant she'd missed her GCSEs and was going to have to stay on a whole extra year while Diana swanned off to Sixth Form College with all the others who'd applied and got their grades. It wasn't fair.

'I was here at the weekends,' she said.

'And I've got a Saturday job, remember?' countered Diana.

Diana worked in one of the souvenir shops on the pier. It sold expensive tat to summer visitors — painted shells and lighthouses and tea towels with Brockhaven written on them and pictures of seagulls and ice cream cones.

'I though you'd have given that up so you'd have more time to swot for the exams.'

Diana sniggered. 'You must be joking. I could pass those Micky Mouse exams with my eyes closed.'

Rowan felt a surge of jealousy. It wasn't

fair. Diana was naturally bright. She, on the other hand, had worked her socks off to get good enough grades in her mocks to secure her a place at Sixth Form College. She'd made herself ill, not eating properly with worry and staying up late to do some last minute revision. And all for what? So she could end up with glandular fever and be forced to take months off school.

'Anyway, the way things are turning out, I don't think I'm even going to bother with sixth form. Who needs more education?'

Rowan restrained herself from yelling down the phone that she did. She couldn't let Diana get even a sniff of how much her flippant remark had infuriated her. It was her secret, how envious she was of a girl whose journey through school had always been so effortless and it made her feel like a bad person that she felt this way.

Besides, knowing Diana, if Rowan yelled at her she'd simply put down the phone. And Rowan needed her. As much as sometimes she hated Diana, she was,

127

after all, her oldest, closest friend. Were everybody else's friendships so complicated, she wondered.

'What will you do then?' she said instead.

There was a pause. Then, 'I can't say why over the phone. It's a secret.' Diana's voice was mysterious. 'We could meet up tomorrow though. Have a wander round the Festival. Then I could let you in on it.'

Rowan had forgotten all about the Brockhaven Festival. And now she was going to miss it to go on a holiday abroad she didn't even want to go on. Two weeks of being trapped on a caravan site with her mum and dad.

'We're off on holiday tomorrow,' Rowan said. 'I won't be back for a fortnight.'

Mum was calling her name from the kitchen. Tea was ready, she said. Rowan held the receiver away from her ear and called out that she'd be there in a minute. Then she resumed her conversation with Diana.

'I can't go away without knowing about this secret of yours.'

'Well you're going to have to.'

Diana was teasing her. Rowan was desperate to know but held back from begging. She still had some pride. It was a bold move. But it worked.

'I'll just say this and the rest will keep till after you get back.'

Diana had relented.

'Thing is,' she said, 'I saw something.'

'Saw what?'

'Something somebody didn't want me to see. And that's all I can say. I've said too much already.'

And with that she rang off. She didn't know it at the time, but that was the last time Rowan was ever to speak to Diana. And she would never set eyes on her again.

$\star$ $\star$ $\star$

'I saw something. Something somebody didn't want me to see.' Casey sat at her desk, trying to collect her scrambled thoughts. What on earth could those words have meant? Did they even have any significance? Rowan Moody certainly

129

seemed to think so or she wouldn't have decided to get in touch with her again.

Casey had written down the words Rowan had insisted Diana had spoken. She'd been staring at them for the last ten minutes, coldly and analytically. She wondered if Rowan had misremembered them. It was more than twenty years ago after all. And besides, by her own admission, she hadn't been well.

'I can't help wondering, Rowan,' she'd asked her, 'why it's taken you so long to report this. I mean, why didn't you say something when you interviewed? After you got back from your holiday?'

'I don't think I was all there back then,' had been her reply. She sounded apologetic. 'Life was moving forward for everybody else, but for me it was standing still and I resented it too much to care about anything or anybody else outside myself. I was horrible to my parents too,' she added.

On top of that, she said, the holiday her parents had hoped would speed her recovery had had the opposite effect. The whole thing had been a disaster because of one thing and another and it had ended up setting her back months. When she'd got back home and was hit with the news that Diana had been murdered, her reactions hadn't been normal. She hadn't been able to stop resenting Diana for dying.

'I'm ashamed to say it now, all these years later,' she said, 'but I felt Diana had died on purpose. So she could make sure I wouldn't ever get better and would never have another friend. I think I just put her out of my mind.'

Casey admired Rowan's honesty. Not many people would own up to such twisted thoughts. But the girl had been sick and lonely and by the sound of it, mired in a deep, undiagnosed depression too.

'Honestly, I hadn't given her final words to me a second thought until you turned up in my classroom and told me you thought you recognised me.'

The first thing Casey did when she'd put the phone down was to make a request for the files appertaining to Diana's case. It was an impulsive gesture but what did she have to lose? She still wasn't fully convinced there was anything in it but she reminded herself the case remained unsolved.

Once Ian Dawlish had been let out of police custody the net had been widened. Although several other people were interviewed and some re-interviewed, none of this led anywhere. It didn't help that Diana went missing on the weekend of the Brockhaven Festival, when the town had more visitors over a weekend than it did for the rest of the year.

Before the end of the day an email popped into her inbox informing her that there were a dozen files on record regarding Diana's case and that she shouldn't discount the fact of there being more at the Coroner's office.

If Casey *was* going to pursue this case, then she was going to have to ask for assistance. There was far too much for one person to investigate single-handedly. But the prospect of knocking on the Super's door and asking if she could put a team together was a daunting one. Would the Commissioner even give permission for the case to be reinvestigated, given such flimsy evidence?

Perhaps the best thing would be simply to drop the whole idea. But how could she, now that Diana's words to Rowan had been so firmly planted in her head? Casey glanced at her watch. It was time to go home. But before she did, she pinged a reply back to the Records Department.

Yes, please, she'd have the files. All twelve of them. And for good measure she also sent an email enquiry to the Coroner. While she waited for them to arrive, she was going to have to retrieve her own files from her memory store. Who knew what she might be able to drag up?

AUGUST 31 1997

There was a charged atmosphere in the room you could almost smell. Everyone was talking at once. On their phones, at each other, gesturing wildly, shaking their heads. Mary Goodwin who was in charge of the tea looked like she'd been crying.

Only Olly Spark seemed oblivious to

the brouhaha. He sat at his desk, squarely, his eyes fixed on his computer monitor, doing what he did best, which was shovelling this morning's snack of choice into his mouth. Salted peanuts, she noticed. Olly would be retiring in two months. Basically, the world could be coming to an end and he wouldn't move a muscle. In his head, he'd retired already.

'What's going on?' Casey said. 'Is this because of Diana?'

She'd caught the news as she'd been driving into work. It was the only news, beamed out on every channel. It was shocking, she had to admit, what had happened to Princess Diana. But it bothered her the way the media had pushed every other piece of news aside to concentrate solely on this tragedy. It was almost like they were enjoying the drama. But what about those poor little boys, her sons?

Olly briefly peeled his eyes off his computer screen. 'Washed up on Keeper's Cove,' he said. 'Serge is looking for you. He wants you down there as soon as. Somebody needs to keep the public away.'

It took a few moments for Olly's words

to compute. When they did, Casey felt like she'd been socked in the jaw.

'Oh God,' she said. 'I thought . . . '

Olly was looking at his screen again.

'They've arrested that lad. The simple one,' he said. 'He's with his mum, waiting for his brief.'

'Who? Ian Dawlish? But that's ridiculous!'

Olly shrugged like it was none of his business and threw another handful of peanuts into his mouth. The amount of snacks he got through in the course of a week was ridiculous. At this rate his retirement would be a short-lived affair. From across the room she saw Barry Hardy almost touching heads with Jeff Taylor. Oh, they'd be loving this, those two.

Rage propelled her in their direction. She was going to have to say something or she'd bust. She'd been assigned to work with D.I. Hardy and D.C. Taylor on the case of the missing girl, Diana Hunter, taking statements from Diana's neighbours. Ian Dawlish lived with his mother, a few doors down from the

Hunters. He was a couple of years older than Diana and they'd known each other all their lives.

According to Diana's mother, Ian Dawlish had a bit of a thing for Diana. He would leave her little presents on the doorstep. An unusual pebble he'd found on the beach; a bunch of flowers — usually from someone else's garden, that sort of thing. Only a couple of weeks before she'd gone missing he'd left her a coconut he'd won at the fair. He was harmless, so Diana's mother said. But he could be a bit annoying and on occasions Diana had had to get sharp with him.

She'd reported all that back, as was her job, and thought that that would be the end of it. Particularly given what she'd passed on to CID about her own dealings with Ian. A couple of times she'd rescued him from the park, where he'd tried to get in with a gang of boys and girls by getting drunk with them and passing out. Of course, they'd all scarpered once whichever of them had been blessed with a conscience had made an anonymous phone call to the police to report where

Ian could be found.

On one occasion she'd come across him down on the beach, trying to resuscitate a seagull who was in a bad way from a ring pull someone had carelessly discarded, unaware or maybe simply careless of the damage those things could do. He'd been in tears, deeply distressed at the sight of the poor bird struggling so pitifully to cling onto life.

She'd taken him home and handed him over to his mother, a little terrier of a woman, as she recalled, who clearly loved her son dearly. Well, she hoped the woman would give them hell once Hardy and Taylor were inside the interview room with her. A boy like that, who cried at the sight of a bird in pain, could never do harm to a human being.

'You're not seriously thinking of charging Ian,' she said.

The two men locked eyes. She'd seen that look pass between them so many times. Whenever she'd dared question them, in fact. It was a fine bromance and she was the interloper.

'This is one for CID, Casey,' Taylor, the

more junior and definitely the more irritating of the two said. 'Shouldn't you been down at Keeper's Cove?'

'Where's the body?'

She addressed her question to his superior officer.

'At the morgue,' DI Hardy replied.

'And they're sure it's murder and not just drowning?'

'First results revealed a lot of damage to the side of her head,' Hardy said. 'And Forensics have taken water samples to look for diatrons.'

If he was trying to baffle her with science, then he'd failed. Diatrons were algae found in the body of water the drowned person had been found in. They could only be ingested through the heart or stomach if the heart was still beating. If Forensics failed to find any in Diana Hunter's body, then it would suggest she'd been killed by another method before being thrown into the water. Perhaps by that blow to the head.

Taylor had been silent for too long. 'Satisfied?' he smirked.

'No. She may have fallen into the water

and died of a cardiac arrest,' Casey said. 'Shouldn't you wait longer for Forensics to draw a proper conclusion? What other forensic evidence do you have that this had anything to do with that boy? Even Diana's mother said he was harmless.'

'First of all, that that boy is an eighteen-year old man,' Hardy replied, drawing himself up to his full height of six foot four. 'Secondly, things have changed. His mum no longer holds that opinion.'

'I didn't know that,' Casey said.

'There's a lot you don't know, Officer,' Taylor said. 'Which is why we're in charge of what happens next and you're not.'

Casey felt a strong desire to punch him. But she knew when she was being deliberately provoked. These two weren't going to win this one. What was that saying? You can either get mad or get even. Well, she knew what she intended doing. As soon as her shift she finished she'd get that application in for a transfer to CID. It had been sitting on her dressing table at home taunting her for far too long.

2018

How hard could detective work be?
Rowan was in the staff room. Everyone
else had left. There was just her and her
laptop. She might not have access to
police computer sites like they did in all
those TV dramas. But she knew people.
Everyone Diana had known in her short
life, Rowan had known too, to a greater or
lesser extent. She was bound to be in a
better position than Detective Inspector
Clunes to try and work out what it was
Diana had on them.

That boy they'd arrested. She still felt
sad when she thought of poor Ian
Dawlish. The village idiot, Diana used to
call him. She was cruel to him. But
Rowan hadn't been much better. She'd
been there with the rest of the gang when
Diana had led the way poking fun at him;
looking on and deeply ashamed that she
wasn't doing anything to stop her.

But however Diana goaded him he still
refused to fight back. Simply put, he
didn't get it. It didn't matter what Diana
said or what she did to him. He was just

happy that she acknowledged him. If there had been as much as a glint of murder in his eye, then Rowan was certain she'd have spotted it.

There was someone else though back then. Not in the gang but always in the background to Diana's life. Her stepbrother. Older than her by only a few months. Quiet, shy, handsome in his own way. Diana had been most put out when he and his father had moved in after her mother had remarried.

What had happened to Carl Crane, she wondered? Was he still living hereabouts? How could she find him, if she wanted to? The answer was obvious. She flipped open her laptop, logged onto Facebook and speedily typed in his name. His image came up immediately. The last time he'd posted anything had been in 2016.

Why was that, she wondered as she skimmed down the rest of the page to see what his friends had written. And there it was. Her answer. She was going to have to give this information to Casey Clunes. Throughout their phone call earlier, Rowan had had a strong suspicion that

Casey was listening to her purely out of politeness. But this *had* to mean something, surely! And maybe when she read it herself she might decide to take Rowan's words more seriously.

3

Casey would never get used to the scent of captive humanity, no matter how many times she visited a prison. The sight of so much decay was depressing. Then there was the smell. The odour of a male prison was made up of equal parts of feet, sweat, stale fags and pent-up testosterone. Add to this the clamour of slamming doors and the almost electrical charge of menace that emanated from the landing and before fifteen minutes was up she had a raging headache and was desperate to leave.

Rowan Moody, it appeared, had decided to do a bit of sleuthing herself. She'd only got as far as social media, but Carl Crane's Facebook page had yielded enough information to intrigue both Rowan and — once she'd relayed the information — Casey herself. Diana Hunter's stepbrother was doing time for GBH.

Didn't that prove he was a violent man, Rowan had demanded. And that he'd probably been a violent teenager? One capable of murdering his stepsister? Casey had struggled to leap to Crane's defence. The time had come to put Diana's case before the Super and suggest reopening the investigation. Much to her surprise, the Super had agreed.

She'd even offered Casey PC Leila Rasheed as an assistant. Okay, so one officer did not a team make. But Casey had never been one to look a gift horse in the mouth and as gift horses went, Leila Rasheed ticked all the boxes. Not only did she possess plenty of stamina, but she was completely unflappable. To say she was easily worth two officers was an understatement.

Before putting in a call to the prison governor to arrange a visit, Casey had familiarised herself with Crane's interview twenty years previously, when he'd been a boy of seventeen. On the weekend of Diana's disappearance — the weekend of the Brockhaven Festival — he'd claimed to be either at home or, once he'd finally emerged from bed after midday, out in the town with his friends. There had been no reason to doubt his story and he hadn't been questioned again.

Since speaking to Rowan, she'd made herself familiar with Crane's colourful past and now had a good grasp of it. This was his first sojourn in prison. But it was by no means his first brush with the law. By all accounts, he described himself as an activist. If there was a demonstration anywhere within a radius of thirty miles, then Crane would be there with his banner and his megaphone. It was during one of these protests that he'd had his first official brush with the law. His second had been a bit more serious and had landed him inside.

He was already seated in the interview room when Casey arrived, being guarded by a burly prison guard, who gave her an indifferent nod as she walked in.

'Hello, Carl,' she said, keeping her voice pleasant.

At her appearance Carl sat up, his pale eyes curious and alert. The muscly arms, covered in tattoos and shaved head were at odds with his small, neat facial features.

'What's this about? This lot don't tell you nothing.'

His voice was stamped with the local accent. Casey suspected it was an affectation, like the tattoos and the pumped upper body. It was part of the armour all inmates with any nous aimed to acquire as soon as possible, in order to avoid being bullied by their co-residents.

'Tell me what you're in for, Carl,' Casey said, gently, once she'd introduced herself.

'It wasn't my fault.'

If she could have had a pound for every time she'd heard that line.

'So who's fault was it?' she asked him. 'On both occasions,' she added.

He shrugged. They'd never got as far as exchanging names, he said. The prison officer sent him a warning. Carl replied with a contemptuous one of his own.

'I was at a demo,' he said. 'Both times. Those things can get a bit lairy. You have to protect yourself.'

'What were you protesting against?'

'First time it was anti-fracking. They said we'd caused some criminal damage.'

Though not a fraction of what the ones doing the fracking were causing, he added.

He'd received a community sentence for that offence, he said.

'Next time it was a big supermarket chain. They wanted to set up two miles away from the local shopping centre. It would have killed everybody else's trade.'

Casey had read the details. This 'local' shopping centre was some twenty-five miles away from Brockhaven. Had he really been concerned by the plight of all those small shopkeepers? Or did he just enjoy a punch up?

'You struck an officer,' she reminded him. 'He ended up in hospital. He now walks with a stick.'

'Look. All I was doing was trying to protect some old bloke next to me. This copper was picking on him. I couldn't let him carry on.'

'So you knocked him unconscious?'

'Mate of yours, was he?'

He received a second glance from the Prison Officer in the corner, accompanied by a verbal warning this time. Casey raised a hand to signal she didn't need any help then turned back to Carl.

'Look, I didn't mean for him to fall and

hit his head like that.' His tone softened. 'But sometimes you have to stick up for your cause, know what I mean? That copper should have been ashamed of himself, defending some big corporate machine that was bent on tearing the heart out of a community.'

'Would you say you were a violent man, when provoked?' Casey said.

He looked aggrieved. Then suspicious. 'What's this really about?' he said.

'How well did you get on with your stepsister, Carl?'

It took him a moment for the penny to drop. When it did he jumped to his feet. The prison officer was there in a moment. Casey could see what would be coming next unless she intervened. Crane would feel provoked and start kicking off. Next, he'd be hauled back to his cell and that would be the end of their little chat.

'Please, Carl,' Casey said. 'No one's accusing you of anything. Just hear me out.'

With some reluctance, he sat back down again.

'You lot took a statement from me all

those years ago,' he said. 'I never laid a finger on her. If anything, *she* was the one you had to look out for.'

Casey pricked up her ears. 'How do you mean?' she asked him.

'Nothing.' Carl's expression suddenly closed down.

Casey repeated her words. No one was accusing him of anything. But just recently something had come to light about Diana. It was possible that she might have been blackmailing someone. And that someone had decided that time was up, and to put an end to it.

'Well I don't know what you think I've got to do with it. I don't know nothing about no blackmailing.'

In that case, what was he implying about Diana?

'Are you telling me the truth, Carl?'

Her question had made him wary.

'Look,' she said. 'I know people say you should never speak ill of the dead. But by all accounts Diana was no angel.' She spoke softly. 'Did she have something on you, Carl?' 'Something it was important no one else discovered?'

149

'I said I don't know what you mean.'

'Perhaps she'd caught you taking money from her mother's purse?'

He gave a contemptuous snort.

'Or did she maybe catch you with a bit of weed?'

'You think that's worth killing someone over, do you? Someone threatening to tell your dad you liked the occasional spliff?'

'I don't know, Carl,' Casey said. 'You tell me. What *is* worth killing someone for?'

He was keeping something from her. Of that, she was certain. All she could do was keep on guessing before sooner or later she'd hit the nail on the head.

'Perhaps you were in a relationship with someone your dad didn't approve of.'

Briefly he raised his eyes from his hands before once more returning his gaze to the table.

'Some girl they didn't think good enough for you?' she said. 'Wrong colour? Wrong class? Wrong religion even? Parents can be funny about stuff like that.'

He gave a laconic shake of the head. 'You're wrong, Officer,' he said. 'There

150

was no girl. There never were girls. Not for me, anyway.'

So then it had to be boys. Diana had discovered he was gay and that he was desperate to hide it.

'You're gay?' she said.

'Took you a while to get there,' he said. 'She found out somehow. But I didn't kill her because of it. In fact, it was the best thing she ever did for me.'

'How come?'

Up until that moment, he said, he'd been confused and ashamed of his sexuality. The thought of no longer having to keep a secret was suddenly liberating.

'I told her to get lost. Said I wasn't so easily blackmailed. Then I marched downstairs, told Dad to turn the telly off and came out to him there and then.'

Once the truth was out about his sexuality, then what possible reason did he have to kill her, he said.

'Right, time up.'

Casey had got what she wanted. She believed him. And now she was sure that Rowan was right. Diana Hunter was a blackmailer. Perhaps Carl had been one of her early victims. Except he hadn't risen to the bait. Maybe others hadn't either. But someone had. Until they'd had enough and decided it was time to put an end to her game.

★　★　★

Casey knew she ought to get back to the Station. But the idea of exchanging one enclosed space for another was unappealing. The smell of the prison still lingered in her nostrils, even after rolling down the car windows and breathing in several lungfuls of air. The only remedy, she concluded, was a walk along the beach. There was nothing like the smell of the sea to kick new life into a body.

She had a sudden idea. Right now this investigation seemed to be all about people. But what about places? Keeper's Cove was a mere half hour's drive away and so far, she hadn't been near the place. So what better opportunity than now? She could spend half an hour there, taking a look round and studying the geography while the sea air worked its magic and buffeted away all traces of the prison.

Maybe then, if she timed it right, she could pick Finlay up from school and drop him home. Remind him he still had a mother. But first, to ease her conscience, she ought to call in and brief Leila on the results of her morning's work.

'So if Diana Hunter's attempts to blackmail her stepbrother had failed, then presumably she didn't give up there,' said Leila, when Casey told her what she'd discovered.

'You have to ask yourself how many other people she tried to get money from,' Casey agreed. 'And how many of them she succeeded with.'

'You mean she could have been successfully blackmailing more than one person?'

Casey didn't know, she said. But what she did know was that they were going to have to start thinking seriously about anyone and everyone in Diana's life who might have had a secret big enough to destroy them, should it ever have got out.

'Someone who would kill in order to make sure it never did,' she said.

It might be a long list, she added.

'Well, we can leave out the natural father,' Leila said. 'He emigrated to Canada after his divorce from Diana's mother. He was well out of her life.'

'We ought to interview Carole Hunter again. And the stepfather. Remind me of his name again.'

She soon came back with a name. Tony Crane. Pillar of respectability etcetera, etcetera, she said. Not that such a reputation had ever succeeded stopping anyone committing murder before, she added.

'Check him out,' Casey said. 'Twenty years ago he never came under any suspicion. But think about it. If Diana *did* have something on him, then there's a good chance others have heard rumours too. Brockhaven's a small place'

'I'm onto it.' Leila paused. 'Gov, what about Ian Dawlish? Are we going to go back and interview him?'

The same question had also occurred to Casey. So far she'd managed to dodge it. The thought of revisiting all that again filled her with dismay. Dawlish would be — what? — thirty-nine, forty by now? Was he still living at home with his mother? Was he happy? Settled? If he was then the chances of him remaining so once the police started probing into his life again grew more remote by the day.

'We should leave him for the time being, Leila,' Casey said. 'Last time he was put under undue pressure to make a confession.'

'I didn't know this.'

Casey apologised for not saying anything sooner. She couldn't explain why not, unless it was because even after all these years the memory of Ian Dawlish, his wrists in handcuffs, shaking with fear and crying for his mother, was still raw in Casey's memory.

'The guys who interviewed him — Barry Hardy and Jeff Taylor — went in hard. Before twenty-four hours were up, he was signing a confession.'

There was a rustle of paper at the other end of the line.

'I haven't located that yet,' Leila said. 'Nor any tapes. Just an initial interview he did with you. At least I think that's your signature at the bottom of his statement.'

'Must be,' Casey said. 'But you won't find any tapes or any other record of his interview with Hardy and Taylor. They would have gone to the CPS and then onto the Independent Police Complaints Commission.'

'Seriously? What happened to those guys?'

'Demoted. I think Hardy resigned later. And Taylor got a transfer to the Met.'

'Good riddance to bad rubbish.'

Casey couldn't disagree with that sentiment. Now that she'd put some distance between herself and the prison, Casey felt herself begin to relax.

'Keep up the good work, Leila,' Casey said. 'I've got to go now.'

'Shall I call you if I discover something interesting?'

'Absolutely,' Casey replied.

Only please, don't let it be too soon, she thought, as up ahead she caught her first glimpse of the sea.

★   ★   ★

Thank God for Doc Martens, thought Casey as she picked her way along the narrow cliff path. The wind was bracing today and seemed to be coming from every direction, whipping her hair around her face and wrapping her coat around her legs. Seagulls wheeled overhead, piercing the air with their maniacal shrieking. Below lay the sea, grey and wrinkled where it met the horizon, foamy and wild where it hit the wall of rock below. The tide was in.

Casey stood as near to the edge as the cordon and the warning signs permitted. She wasn't about to sacrifice her life just to get a good enough look at the drop. But she needed to fix in her mind how much or how little of the town below could be seen from up here, and by the same token, how much of this spot was visible from the town. Even on a clear day like today, the answer was very little.

Few people came up here these days. There were too many stories of lost dogs and people suddenly slipping as the cliff edge crumbled beneath their feet. Erosion was happening so fast that it was a commonly held view that sooner rather than later the entire wall of cliffs would fall into the sea and disappear forever.

Nowadays, the place was full of warning signs, but twenty years ago the signs were fewer. Even back then, though, it was still relatively off the beaten track. And on the weekend of the local fair the place would have been even more isolated. It would have been a good weekend for a murder without witnesses.

From the material available, Casey had committed to memory everything she needed to know about the day Diana Hunter had gone missing. She'd failed to arrive home on the evening of Saturday July 26, after leaving the house in the morning to go to her job on the pier.

Before she left, she told her mum she'd probably be later back than usual because someone she knew was performing on the stage around half six. But she definitely wouldn't be later than nine, she insisted, because there was something on TV she wanted to watch.

As part of the festival, Pat and Tony had volunteered to run a vintage clothes sale the following day, so were stuck at home sorting and labelling all the items they'd had dumped on them by the generous residents of Brockhaven. By the time they'd finished, so their statements had read at the time, they were too exhausted to do anything more than sit in front of the TV with a bottle of wine, where they'd both fallen asleep.

When Carl arrived home round half eleven, along with a couple of his mates who'd missed their bus home and needed a bed for the night, they naturally asked him if he'd seen his stepsister in the market square where they'd been for the last four hours.

It was when Carl said he hadn't seen hide or hair of her all day that they first tried to contact Jenn Stone, who ran 'Pierless Gifts' where Diana worked at the weekend. When no one picked up, they tried ringing round all her friends. Of course, this was back in the day when the only people who carried mobile phones were city types. So with everyone out on the town, they'd have received few answers on that Saturday night. It was after so many fruitless enquiries that they decided to ring the police.

Casey's phone emitted a muffled ringing from inside her coat pocket. It was Leila. As usual, she cut straight to the chase.

'Boss,' she said. 'That conversation you had with Rowan Moody. About the last time she spoke to Diana. She said that she'd told Diana she wouldn't be able to see her next day because they were off on holiday, right?'

'That's correct.'

'It's just, well, I've been reading back through the statement Jenn Stone gave. She ran the shop where Diana worked.'

'Yes. Pierless Gifts. Peerless name too,' Casey said.

'I don't know why it wasn't picked up at the time,' Leila said, her tone urgent. 'But she says that roundabout lunchtime on that Saturday, someone came to the shop looking for Diana. A friend of hers, she said.'

'Did she say who it was?'

'No. But she described a well-spoken, very pale, skinny girl with long, dark hair.

Said she looked like she hadn't been out of the house in months.'

It was a perfect description of Rowan as Casey herself would have described her when she'd interviewed her a couple of weeks later.

'What did she want?'

'She said the girl wanted to know if Diana could come to lunch. But Jenn Stone said they were being pulled out of the shop by the customers and Diana's lunch break was going to have to wait till things calmed down.'

Casey turned this over in her mind. So Rowan had lied not only twenty years ago in her statement, but just recently, over the phone to Casey. What else had she lied about, Casey asked herself.

'Look, I'm out at Keeper's Cove, Leila. But I'm just about to leave for St Bede's to pick Finlay up,' she said. 'Rowan's bound to be somewhere in the building. I think the two of us need to have another little chat.'

4

Casey got to the school gates just as the children had been set free. Amongst the flood of children streaming her way, she spotted Finlay immediately. He reminded her so much of Dom. Not just physically, although these last few months he'd shot up and was now taller than she was. His mannerisms were the same too. Right now, he was engrossed in conversation with another boy, alternately stabbing the air to make a point and nodding his head enthusiastically in agreement with something the other boy said.

Maybe it was a skill she'd developed in her police training, or maybe she'd just been born vigilant. But whichever it was, her vigilance didn't seem to be a trait Finlay had inherited. Right now he was oblivious to everything else going on around him, despite the fact that she was only feet away. When she was close enough to stand on his toes he finally

162

looked up and saw her.

'Mum! What you doing here?'

'I've come to pick you up,' she said, resisting the temptation to give him a big hug. 'But first I need to speak to someone so perhaps you can wait in the car till I'm ready?'

She risked a friendly smile in the direction of his companion and the friend smiled back. Was it too much to expect an introduction? Honestly her son's manners were appalling.

'But Mum, I don't want picking up,' said an aggrieved Finlay. 'I'm going to Stephen's for tea and to do our project. And then his mum's bringing me back home.'

Casey slapped her forehead as if she'd suddenly remembered.

'Of course,' she said, covering up her disappointment at being denied some rare one-to-one time with Finlay. 'In that case, I'll let you guys get on.'

As she watched them walk away she called out, 'Nice to meet you Stephen. And don't forget to say thanks for having me to Stephen's mum, Finn.'

But they'd already forgotten about her.

Casey was here on police business but all the way in the car she'd been hoping she wouldn't have to flash her ID. Fortunately, at reception she was immediately recognised as that police officer who'd visited before, so when she asked if she could have a word with Miss Moody, she was buzzed through without a second glance.

Through the classroom window, Casey saw Rowan Moody deep in conversation with Sally Seddon. Or rather Sally Seddon was holding forth, waving some sheets of paper in the air while Rowan sat in stiff silence at her desk. She was gripping a pencil between her two hands, Casey noticed, rather as if she were visualizing her head of department's neck and she was about to snap it in two.

When Casey gave a brisk rap at the door before entering, both women looked up simultaneously; Rowan with relief and Sally Seddon with curiosity. Somehow Casey was going to have to get rid of the latter before she could speak to Rowan in confidence.

'What a pleasure to see you again, Mrs — er — Clunes.' Sally Seddon stepped forward to greet her, her hand outstretched.

Casey couldn't fault the woman for remembering her surname. Though she rather balked at the Mrs, having always been a Ms when she wasn't being an Inspector. She shook her hand, pleasantly.

'To what do we owe the pleasure?' Sally Seddon said.

Casey turned to Rowan. 'Actually, it's Rowan I need to speak to.' she said.

'Sure,' Rowan said, sitting up. 'I'm not going anywhere.'

Sally Seddon didn't even try to hide her inquisitiveness. Casey wouldn't have been surprised to see her nose and ears start twitching.

'What's this about, Mrs Clunes? Because if it's something to do with your son then maybe, since I'm here and as I'm head of department . . . '

'This is nothing to do with Finlay, Ms Seddon,' Casey said, firmly. 'It's a private matter.'

Ms Seddon's eyes darted back and

forth between Rowan and Casey several times. When it became clear that she'd get no more information from either of them, she collected her stuff from the table and bustled out of the room, her cheerful goodbye thinly veiling her disappointment at being left out of the loop.

'Thank God she's gone!' Rowan sat back in her chair, suddenly relaxed. 'What is it, Casey?' she said. 'Is it about Diana?'

'It shouldn't take a minute,' Casey said, though she was nowhere near sure about that. 'I just need to put something to you.'

'Go ahead.' Rowan looked intrigued.

'On the day Diana Hunter went missing, you paid a visit to Pierless Gifts where she had a Saturday job and asked the shop owner if Diana was around.'

'Did I? I can't remember.'

'The owner of the shop described someone remarkably similar to you in her statement. Until now, no one had paid it much attention.'

Rowan put her hand to her mouth. What else was she covering up, Casey wondered?

'You told me that on the phone you'd

informed Diana you'd be going on holiday on the Saturday so you'd have no time to meet up with her.'

'That's right.'

'And you also told me that after that phone call you never spoke to her again.'

'And that was the truth. I *didn't* speak to her after that phone call.'

'Well someone's lying, Rowan,' Casey said. 'Who is it? The shop owner, or you?'

Rowan appeared to be tussling with her thoughts.

'Neither of us was lying,' she said, unable to look Casey in the eye. 'I just left this bit out, that's all.'

'So you're not denying you went down to the pier with the intention of seeing Diana.'

'No I'm not.' Her voice was strained. 'But I didn't see her and I didn't speak to her.' She raised her gaze from her desk and met Casey's eyes. 'I'm sorry I misled you.'

'Actually, you misled me twice,' Casey reminded her. 'The first time was twenty years ago, when you got back from holiday and I came to your house to speak to you. You were with your mother, in your bedroom.'

'And that was the reason I said what I said back then, don't you see?'

No, Casey didn't see. Perhaps Rowan would care to explain.

'The day we went on holiday we were due to leave for the airport round about five. Mum and Dad wanted to catch the parade but said I should stay home and rest because the journey was bound to take it out of me.'

She didn't stay home, though, she said. Instead she took the opportunity to pay Diana a visit.

'I was curious to find out what she had to tell me about whatever it was she'd seen and was being so secretive about,' she said. 'But when I got down there her boss was in a mood and told me she couldn't spare Diana so I came back home.'

If she'd told Casey the truth, then her Mum would have been angry with her. Especially since her jaunt down to the pier and back had made her quite ill again and the flight had been a nightmare, not to mention pretty much the rest of the holiday.

'They'd been so looking forward to that holiday,' Rowan said. 'And I spoiled it for them. I should have owned up but I was too much of a coward to say I'd disobeyed them.'

So then, she added, since she'd told Casey this lie once, she thought it would seem odd, like she was hiding something, if she changed her story. It was cowardly of her, she said, and she was sorry. Casey turned everything over in her mind. It all sounded plausible, she had to admit.

'Actually, I did have a witness, as a matter of fact,' Rowan said, rather as if the memory had surprised her. 'Though she might have died of old age by now.'

It was her old music teacher, she said. Mrs Lightfoot, the wife of the head teacher at St Bede's.

'Not the present head, obviously,' she went on. 'I mean Dr Lightfoot who retired when we were in Year Eight or Nine.'

Rowan's mum used to take her to piano lessons at the Lightfoots' house for about two years, she told Casey.

'I hated it,' Rowan said. 'I begged Mum so often to stop making me go that in the end I wore her down.'

Mrs Lightfoot was very cross about it, apparently. It was as if she took it as a personal slight.

'When I saw her peering through the window of the shop I pretended I hadn't seen her,' she said. 'I was terrified that if I caught her eye she'd pin me up against a wall and force me to start piano lessons again.'

Rowan gave a chuckle. It was so infectious that Casey joined in.

'She sounds like a monster,' she said.

'She was,' Rowan said. 'She used to yell 'F sharp' or 'B flat' randomly. Once she threatened to cut my fingernails if I didn't do them myself.'

Casey gave a grimace. 'Do you still play?' she said.

'You're joking! I never got beyond 'Turkey in the Straw'.'

'Two years, did you say? Strikes me you did well to last that long!'

Rowan gave a nod of agreement. 'Although thinking about it now, she might actually have taught me a valuable lesson,' she said.

Casey was intrigued to find out what that might be.

'That good teaching is about inspiring children, not brow-beating them,' she said.

Casey didn't think she could argue with that.

★ ★ ★

Memory was a funny thing. In all these years, Rowan hadn't given Mrs Lightfoot a second thought. But something about that conversation with the DI had jogged her memory. And now, as she ploughed through her marking, she was unable to get the wretched woman out of her head.

How she'd hated those piano lessons. She'd plead headache, tummy ache, a strained wrist, absolutely anything to get out of it. But no, week on week Mum would march her to the Lightfoots for an hour of torture while she went off to change her library books. It had taken tears and tantrums in the end to get

Mum to let her leave.

Dad was more sympathetic. He hated seeing her upset and to be fair, Rowan played on her ability to wrap him round her little finger. He'd taken her along once or twice himself and understood perfectly her reasons for not wanting to continue.

'I pity her poor husband,' she remembered him once saying to Mum. 'The woman terrifies me.'

She'd terrified Rowan too, although when her mother questioned her about what she found so terrifying she'd never been able to bring herself to say why. Her mother, who was far stricter with her than her father had ever been, would accuse her of making things up just so she wouldn't have to go again.

The truth was, she'd just never felt safe there. Mrs Lightfoot may have been polite and smiling when Mum dropped her off and picked her up. But for that hour in-between she was a tyrant, perpetually undermining Rowan's confidence with her sarcastic remarks.

Thinking about it, her teaching methods rather put her in mind of those of

Sally Seddon. Perhaps the similarity between the two women was the reason Sally rubbed her up the wrong way as much as she did.

'I thought you might be in need of this.'

When Rowan looked up and saw Sally Seddon in the doorway bearing two steaming mugs of coffee, she almost jumped out of her skin. It was almost as if just thinking about the woman had conjured her up. She was immediately suspicious. Sally had never made her a cup of coffee in all the time she'd taught at the school.

'How far have you got?' Sally picked up one of the scripts on Rowan's desk and flicked through the pages in a leisurely fashion.

Actually, she hadn't got very far at all, as Sally would find out if she continued to poke about on her desk like that. Rowan had been tasked with the duty of going through the papers Sally had already marked, to see if she agreed with the marks she'd allocated. It was a way of making sure that in a mock A-level exam the students were all being marked according to the same criteria.

Going on the ten or so scripts she'd managed to tackle after the DI's departure, she was now firmly of the opinion that Sally had been far too stringent in her marking. But her heart was heavy with the prospect of having to tell her so. Sally Seddon couldn't abide being wrong. She was never going to let Rowan forget that not only was she older than her and superior in status, but that once upon a time she'd been her English teacher.

'So-so,' said Rowan, putting off the moment when she was going to have to tell Sally that she thought her marks were too harsh.

In her head, she began to trawl through the stock of diplomatic phrases she kept specifically for her encounters with Sally. But before she could locate the exact one she needed, Sally cut in.

'What did she want then? The lady detective?'

It amused Rowan mildly that Sally should feel the need to stipulate Casey's gender.

'Oh, nothing. Nothing to do with

school anyway,' she murmured.

Sally had brushed the papers Sally had marked to one side to make a space for herself on the desk, where she now perched.

'Have you been the victim of a crime?' She spoke with concern in her eyes.

'No!'

'Or perhaps you're a suspect!'

Rowan giggled nervously. Sally's concerned expression was replaced with one of exasperation.

'Oh come on, Rowan,' she said. 'There's no need to be so secretive. And anyway, I won't tell anyone.'

Rowan felt like a butterfly might feel once it had been netted. Trapped. A sudden crazy idea dropped into her head. If she gave Sally even a tiny bit of information about the police's reawakened interest in Diana's murder, then she might suddenly take Rowan's criticism more amiably than if she refused to give her any information at all.

She was minded of the fact that she was due a performance review shortly and that, as her line manager, Sally could make things very difficult for her. Besides, it was only a matter of time before the media picked up on the fact that Diana's case had been reopened.

'Well, if I tell you,' she said, beginning hesitantly, 'You must promise me not to breathe a word of it.'

Sally's face was inches away from her own. She could see the flecks of hazel in her eyes and the splatter of broken veins on her cheeks that the concealer she'd so liberally appeared failed to hide.

'Do you remember Diana Hunter?' she said.

★   ★   ★

It had come as such a shock, hearing that dreadful girl's name after all these years. For a moment, Sally thought she might have been about to pass out. If Rowan hadn't put her hand out and grabbed hold of her arm at just the right moment, then she jolly well may have done.

She'd passed off her funny turn with a remark about missing lunch and thankfully Rowan hadn't noticed. Far too busy blethering on about the discrepancy in their marking. She'd let the girl get away with it in the end. Given her her moment of glory. Truth was, her head was all over the place at the mention of Diana Hunter's name.

It was no use. She was going to have to ring him. It wasn't fair that she should carry this burden alone. Did he have the same phone number, Sally wondered? Their affair had long been over but she still had her old red address book with the gilt lettering on the front cover.

There was no mobile number in it, just the landline number, unfortunately. She was taking a risk by ringing it. But it was a risk she was just going to have to take. Carefully, she dialled the number. Half-way through, she keyed in the wrong one and had to start again. Damn! She needed to calm down. She tried again, this time taking it slowly. When she heard it ringing at the other end she almost put it down. But before she got that far, someone answered. It was him.

'Paul Lightfoot speaking. Good evening.'
She barely recognised his voice. It was

the voice of an old man, she thought.

'Hello.' He spoke again.

She needed to find her own voice. But what to say? In the end there was only one thing *to* say. It was a cliché beloved of bad drama. And Sally, who, as a lover of the great dramatists from Shakespeare onward, loathed a cliché more than she loathed factory-made bread, found herself saying it.

'It's me,' she murmured. 'We need to talk.'

★ ★ ★

He could simply have put the phone down. It wasn't as if there'd been anything between them this past twenty years. He was an old man now. A good ten years older than she was and it wasn't as if she'd been any spring chicken when they'd started their affair. But there was an urgency in her voice. A teacher's command. And he was curious.

'Who was that?'

Anne had been clearing up after dinner. She came bustling out of the kitchen, shaking out the tea towel with her Marigold-clad hands, her small eyes full of suspicion. All these years and she still didn't feel she could trust him. Although *that* worked both ways.

'It was Tommo,' he said, the lie leaving his lips as smooth as a newly laid egg. 'From the History Society. Needs to bend my ear about something.'

'You're not going out? I thought we'd watch that Morse repeat.'

He was already reaching for his coat. Best thing was not to get sucked into a conversation. Otherwise before too long it would turn into an argument. Then heaven only knew where that would lead. He'd be apologising till the small hours.

'I won't be long,' he said. 'Just a half or two.'

He'd seen this particular repeat at least twice, anyway, he added, winding his scarf around his neck.

'Oh well, in that case,' Anne sighed, 'I'll sit through it on my own. Though no doubt I'll fall asleep halfway through.'

She'd had a stream of particularly dim pupils all afternoon and quite frankly she was exhausted, she said. Half of them still hadn't grasped where middle C was yet. There was more of this, but he'd stopped listening. He simply nodded sympathetically and reached for his keys. Then, with a nod in her direction, he opened the front door and was gone.

She waited less than a minute before tossing the tea towel onto the floor and peeling off her Marigolds. Then she lifted the receiver and dialled 1471. She didn't recognise the number. But she recognised that glint in Paul's eye. And she wasn't stupid.

'Well,' she said aloud to the cat, who was winding himself around her legs in the hope of being given a few more scraps of food. 'Two can play at that game.'

She would give him fifteen minutes. He was on foot and Brockhaven was a small town. As soon as the clock in the hall chimed the quarter hour she'd get in her car and find him. Which of the six pubs within walking distance would you take your lady friend to, she asked herself? Unless they'd planned that she would pick him up some place and the two of them would drive out of town so as not to be discovered together. They could, of course, go back to her place.

She stood in the hallway, ignoring Ginger's mewling, her eyes fixed on the clock. She could feel the rush of adrenaline coursing through her body. She was poised. Tense. Ready for anything. When the clock struck the quarter she let go of the breath she'd been holding onto in her excitement.

'Time to go, Ginger,' she murmured, as she let herself out of the house.

5

Rowan was lounging by the sink in the staffroom kitchen, relishing the fact that for her, Wednesdays always began with a double free period. Everyone else bar one or two other staff members had trotted off to class and silence had finally descended.

Not total silence of course. The ancient staff kettle, valiantly battling against layers of lime scale, groaned and wheezed its way towards boiling point. On the other side of the kitchen wall, pages rustled, throats cleared and fingers tapped out lesson plans on keyboards. Further away still were the classroom sounds; the slamming of desk lids, a teacher's raised command, the low-level hum of children's babble interspersed with an occasional sputtering salvo of unruly noise.

Her meditation was suddenly ruptured by a clatter of footsteps up the stairs. It came to a sudden halt on the other side of the staffroom door, before it burst open to reveal the school secretary, Janice. She looked, Rowan thought, even more aggrieved than she usually did whenever something forced her away from the comfort of her office.

'Rowan,' she panted, her face red from exertion. 'You need to get to Sally's class. She's not turned up for her Year Tens and mayhem's descending.'

'Is she sick?' asked Rowan.

Sally Seddon was never sick. Although there'd been a moment, yesterday, when Rowan wondered if she might be having some sort of turn. In fact, she'd been so worried that Sally might have been about to topple off the desk where she'd perched herself while they compared scripts, that Rowan had shot out a hand and grabbed her by the wrist to stop her falling. Talk about awkward. But Sally hadn't seemed to notice.

'Well, if she is, she hasn't bothered to ring in and report it,' Janice said, once she'd got her breath back. 'And she's on a full timetable today. I don't know how I'm expected to find cover at such short notice.'

Rowan didn't need to hear any of this. Sally Seddon's Year Tens were notorious. Pushing all thoughts of her head of department's mysterious absence to one side, Rowan set about channelling her energy into thinking of something engaging and relevant enough to occupy them for the next eighty minutes. Then, having found the material she needed and thrown it into her briefcase, she gave a last, lingering glance at the kettle. Wouldn't you just know it. Finally, it had coughed and wheezed its way up to boiling point. So much for her free period.

★   ★   ★

The first thing she saw when she opened her eyes was the cat flap. Ridiculous, when she didn't even have a cat. Her head was banging. When she tried to raise it from the floor, the dull olive green of the carpet she was lying on began to come into focus.

Sally raised her hand to her head. Blood. Not the deep, red, flowing sort. But sticky, almost brown. She attempted to get up. But even the slightest weight on her hands jarred her shoulder and she immediately sank back down. She'd be better off staying where she was, she decided, and closed her eyes again.

All her body wanted was rest but it seemed her mind had decided otherwise. Pictures and shapes slowly began to form in her memory. People's voices. The chink of glasses and background chatter. They were in The Anchor, tucked away in the Snug where occasional snatches of sound reached them from the Lounge, where the weekly quiz was taking place. They sat opposite one another. Once upon a time they would have sat side by side, struggling to keep their hands off each other.

'Why on earth did you phone my house?'

She didn't recognise anything of the Paul she'd once loved. He looked old. He *was* old, she reminded herself. Old and weary, as if all joy had leeched out of him. Was that how she looked too, these days?

When they'd started their affair all those years ago she'd been the age Rowan Moody was now. A young teacher at the

185

beginning of her career. He'd been in his prime. When he walked into a room the children sat up straight. The staff too. How it had flattered her when he sought her out. And the secrecy of what they both knew they were entering into added another layer of intrigue.

'I can just imagine Anne's face if I'd turned up at your house and rung your front doorbell,' she snarled. 'How is dear Anne these days? Still making your life a misery, is she?'

When he failed to answer she guessed she'd hit the nail on the head. What a coward he was, to stay so long with a woman he didn't love. Just because it was convenient. He hadn't deserved her own devotion.

'What do you want, Sally?'

He was half way through his pint of beer already. She told him he ought to take it easy because he needed a clear head to listen to what she had to say. And then she told him straight.

'The police,' she said. 'They've reopened the case on Diana Hunter.'

His tired, red-rimmed eyes opened

wider. He'd suddenly woken up.

'Why now? Have they found any new evidence? Have they spoken to you? What have you told them?'

He was tripping over himself with all these questions.

'Oh, don't worry. They know nothing about me. I was never interviewed the first time, remember?'

'Do you think they might want to speak to me?'

They were speaking to everyone who'd had some sort of connection with the girl, she told him.

'You were headmaster at the time. You gave that sweet little speech to the press about what a likeable, good-natured girl she was and how much she'd contributed to student life.'

'I'm sure it will be easy for you to speak to the police with a clear conscience and regurgitate the same rubbish if you have nothing to fear from them, Paul,' she said. 'And you don't, do you?'

She watched him sink the rest of his drink.

'Finish your drink and I'll get us

another,' he said, quickly getting to his feet without replying.

Had he been drinking before he got here? Or was that unsteadiness something he'd acquired since they'd parted ways? She was drinking gin and tonic. She tossed back what was left in her glass and requested the same again.

While he was at the bar she thought back to when the blackmail had started. It had been a foolish thing to do, of course, in a public place. Her classroom, as she recalled. Or maybe it was in the school office. She could no longer remember all the details. They thought they were the only ones sharing that embrace. But they'd been wrong.

She remembered Diana's footsteps coming up behind her as she made her way to her car, once Paul and she had disentangled themselves. She'd seen everything, Diana said. And if Sally didn't give her money then she would pay a visit to the headmaster's wife and tell her what she'd seen.

She should have stood up to her immediately. But she was young and she was foolish and some misplaced sense of loyalty to Paul Lightfoot's reputation and that of the school made her an easy target. So she asked Diana what she wanted and Diana told her.

Her parents wanted her to go to Sixth Form College, she said, and then get a job in the bank. But she wasn't interested in doing her A-levels or rotting in Brockhaven for the rest of her life. Other kids, the ones with the money, went travelling. Australia, the Far East, anywhere abroad. She wanted a taste of adventure too. But for that she needed money.

Sally paid up dutifully, fool that she was. For weeks, she didn't say a thing to Paul about what was going on. But then one night, when the money she'd shelled out had begun to mount up, she'd spilled it all out. She hoped he'd do something. What exactly, she didn't know. She just needed him to take control.

But he just crumbled. He was terrified. Talked on and on about what it would do to his reputation if any of this got out. Then he brought up his marriage and how it would destroy it. It was in that moment that she fell out of love with him. When he offered to reimburse her everything she'd already shelled out to keep Diana quiet she accepted, feigning gratitude.

Deep down she felt it was only what she was owed. So she kept his money and next time Diana came knocking at her classroom door she told her that as far as she was concerned she could whistle for any more money from her.

She'd learned enough about the girl to know that she wouldn't leave it there. Had she gone to Paul's wife, like she'd threatened? If she had, then her visit appeared to have had little effect. They were still together and remained together to this day. The knowledge that this was the case left her curiously unaffected. The man she thought she'd loved and who loved her had let her down. As far as she was concerned the two of them were finished.

There was a queue at the bar. She wasn't interested in staying longer. She'd said her piece. Reaching for her bag and jacket and making as little noise possible, she rose from the table and slipped out of the side entrance. A walk home would do her good. The streets were empty tonight. Brockhaven was a lazy little town unless it was the summer season. Nothing much ever happened here till Thursday night when the weekend's carousing began.

Perhaps she ought to have taken more care and looked behind her. But she hadn't thought there was anything to be afraid of. Had she heard footsteps? Or was she only imagining them to fit her story as she lay here, staring at the cat flap moving in and out of vision while she grew gradually colder and stiffer and less and less able to move?

She forced herself to think harder. When she did, last night's walk home began to take a clearer shape. She was starting to remember. She'd told herself it was an echo, nothing more. Footsteps stopping when she stopped. Tap-tap-tapping when when she started walking again. She remembered finally reaching her front door, in a hurry to get on the other side of it. And how her nerves made her fingers awkward, as, in the dark, she scrabbled in her bag for her keys.

She remembered too her relief at finally locating them, slipping the key into the keyhole and finally crossing the threshold. But her relief was short-lived. A shadow swept over her, like a dark cape. A hand pressed hard in the small of her back and she felt a blow to her head. The last thing she was aware of as she went down was the faint scent of lavender. Then, nothing at all.

And now whoever it was was back again. Pushing hard against her door, calling her name loud and insistently. And this time, she was certain they would kill her.

★   ★   ★

He didn't know what to do. Anne wasn't home when he got back from the pub, irate that Sally had left him there alone. He sat at the kitchen table, listening to the ticking of the clock on the wall, pouring himself one whisky and then another and thinking what a mess he'd made of his life. Sally was right. He was a coward. But exactly how big a coward, only he knew. Because he'd known for twenty years what Anne had done. And in all this time he'd done nothing about it. Just to save his own skin.

She'd been furious when he confessed to his affair. Not so much because she thought another woman had taken her place in his affections. But because if got out, she said, then not only would he lose his job, but he'd lose his reputation too. They'd have to move. And what about her own reputation, too? Who would entrust their children to someone whose husband was an adulterer?

He hadn't known what to do to calm her down. Everything he said or did only made her more furious. She seemed incapable of sitting still and several times he caught her watching him with murder in her eyes. For weeks after his confession he felt unable to turn his back on her and he was too terrified to sleep. He wrote to Sally. Told her to take care. He was afraid that Anne might confront her, he said. She never wrote back. He didn't blame her.

A month or so after he'd made his

confession, Anne's mood suddenly lightened. When out of nowhere she told him she thought they ought to do a bit of redecorating, he took it as a sign that she'd forgiven him. A clean sweep and all that. He volunteered to help.

He discovered it screwed up at the back of the cupboard in the garage where he kept his paintbrushes. It was a single shoe. A girl's shoe. Tan in colour with a small heel. Size 5. There was stain inside. Like old blood.

He remembered how his own blood had run cold. Because only the weekend before, Diana Hunter's body had been found washed up at Keeper's Cove. He could have thrown the shoe away. If he had, then he wouldn't have to do what he knew he needed to do now.

Paul poured himself a final drink. Sally Seddon's life was very likely under threat right now. He'd been too much of a coward to go to the police and hand over that girl's shoe all those years ago. Stupid, too. Because if he'd done that then he'd have got off scot-free. After all, having an affair wasn't illegal, not in this country at least. But concealing evidence of a murder. Well, that was another thing altogether. But he was ready to take his punishment.

★ ★ ★

The head wound wasn't deep and nothing was broken, but the hospital were keeping Sally under observation for now, just in case. Rowan sat by her bed, feeling awkward. She was used to seeing her head of department in full slap and dressed to the nines. In her nightdress, tucked up in her narrow hospital bed, face bare of a single trace of make up, she looked vulnerable.

She looked more likeable somehow too. Which was why Rowan had found herself inviting Sally to come and stay at hers for a few days till she got properly better. Whatever had happened to her had obviously given her a bad shock and she'd readily accepted Rowan's invitation. The fact that her house was now a crime scene had no doubt contributed to her ready acceptance.

'I can't thank you enough for giving up

your lunch break to come and check on me like you did,' Sally said. 'Otherwise I'd still be there now.'

'Please, don't try to sit up,' Rowan said, as an agitated Sally struggled to raise her head from her pillow. 'The police said they'd be here shortly to interview you. You might as well rest till then.'

Sally's head flopped back on the pillow and she closed her eyes. She looked exhausted.

'Do you have any idea who could have done this to you?' Rowan couldn't stop herself from asking.

A single tear trickled from beneath Sally's eyelid. She gave a weak nod.

'I wondered if it might be him at first,' she said. 'But I should have guessed. He never was a man who could stand up for himself. And he doesn't wear lavender perfume.'

★ ★ ★

Casey had been on her way out when the duty sergeant stopped her. A Dr Paul Lightfoot needed to have a word with someone senior who was working on the Diana Hunter reinvestigation, he said. Casey had been intrigued. As far as she knew, the fact that the case had been re-opened was still only known to a handful of people.

He'd been offered a seat in one of the waiting areas but was obviously too distraught to sit down. He looked wild-eyed and like a man who'd had no sleep. Even from this distance, she could smell the alcohol on his breath.

'Doctor Lightfoot,' she said, in her pleasantest voice.

He spun round, his hands stiff by his side, like a frightened man desperate to contain his fear.

'My wife murdered Diana Hunter,' he said. 'And I suspect she's tried to do the same to a woman called Sally Seddon.'

⋆　⋆　⋆

'She said she did it for him. For their marriage. And to save his reputation.'

Two months had passed. Casey thought it only right to pay Rowan a call in order to inform her that Anne Lightfoot had been charged with Diana Hunter's murder.

Rowan looked shocked.

'How did she kill her?' she asked.

'She went to her work, lured her to the cliffs. Diana must have made the mistake of turning her back on Anne. She reached for a piece of rock, struck her on the head, then rolled her over the edge of the cliff into the water below.'

'No!' Rowan put her hands to her ears, as if shutting out the truth meant it had never happened. 'Poor Diana.'

Casey gave her time to take it all in. It was going to be hard for her, coming to terms with all of this.

'So my memory was correct,' Rowan said, after a while. 'I *did* see Mrs Lightfoot on the pier that day, looking in through the window.'

Casey nodded.

'And you're saying Dr Lightfoot was having a torrid affair with Sally Seddon? *Our* Sally Seddon?'

Rowan was obviously struggling to get her head round the fact that once upon a time Sally Seddon had had a sex life.

'So this was the secret Diana wanted to

share with me,' Rowan said.

'I guess so,' said Casey. 'Maybe if she'd gone to Paul Lightfoot instead of to his wife her story would have ended differently.'

'She may have lived, you mean?'

'It's my guess that he'd have paid up. Anything for a quiet life.'

There was always a chance, of course, that Diana may have decided to try her luck elsewhere once she realised how easy it was to make money out of people's secrets. And maybe the next person or the one of after that, or the one after that, would have decided to put to a stop to it after a while. She didn't say as much, however.

'What will you do now, Rowan? A little bird tells me Sally Seddon's on extended sick leave.'

The little bird, in fact, was Finlay, delighted that his wacky stories were no longer being torn to shreds and that English lessons had suddenly got fun again.

'The school needs an acting head of department and people say I should apply,' Rowan said. 'Only I don't know.

I'm not sure I want to stay at St Bede's any longer. Or even in Brockhaven.'

Casey could understand that. Sometimes a new start could be the answer.

'She didn't deserve it you know,' Rowan added. 'Whatever she got up to.'

'She was young. Foolish. Headstrong.'

'If I'd have been around at the time I would have talked her out of it,' Rowan said.

'Please, don't blame yourself, Rowan. None of this had anything to do with you.'

'No. I know. Only. I can't help but think that if I'd been a better friend.'

Casey didn't want to leave Rowan like this. But Finlay was waiting in the playground for her. Ten minutes, she'd told him, that's all I need. That had been half an hour ago.

'You know,' she said. 'Don't decide anything right now. About applying for promotion. In fact, it might be a good idea to let someone else take over from Sally temporarily.'

Rowan came out of her trance. Casey could almost feel her bristling at the very idea.

'Is that really your advice?' she said, annoyed.

Casey chuckled. 'No,' she said. 'I just wanted to see your reaction. And now I have it.'

'For a police officer you'd make a great life coach,' said Rowan.

'And you'll make a brilliant head of department when the time comes,' Casey said.

A very irate Finlay was knocking on the classroom window. It was time to go home.

After Phoebe

1

Vonny Quinn told herself no one would recognise her. Twenty years was a long time. People moved on. Those that remained made new memories. Fundamentally, people were only interested in themselves anyway, Vonny told herself as she slipped past the Porter's Lodge of St Rita's College. Nobody's looking at you, Quinn. Nobody cares.

Outside these walls was the city of Oxford, which, these days, was much like any other city but with taller spires and more tourists. Inside, however, little had changed. The same motley collection of buildings that were here when she left were here still.

The original elegant two-storey hall, where students and fellows took their meals still dominated, posing stylishly against a backdrop of trees and manicured lawns. But other buildings had been added over the years. Some stood at odd angles to the main house, giving a higgledy-piggledy effect, with little thought to how they fitted into their more gracious surroundings.

The ugliest building of all was Vonny's old student house, unimaginatively called New House. The sixties-built concrete block — visible from the Old Library where she stood — was six storeys high. She thought she was prepared for how she'd feel being back there. But she was nowhere near ready. The very sight of New House lent a grey chill to the day, even though the sun was bright this morning and white, fluffy clouds straight out of a Simpsons' cartoon dotted the blue sky. She shivered, shifting her gaze away.

From this spot, the river was out of sight. Even though she could neither see it nor hear it, thanks to the noise of traffic rumbling by, she knew it was there, snaking its way through the college grounds. No doubt students still punted down it in the summer months, had picnics, fell in love, dreamed about a life with no exams and speculated upon a brilliant future, just as she'd done herself. Well, just look where that had got her.

'Know where you're heading with that mop and bucket?'

A man's voice, tinged with an Oxfordshire burr, broke Vonny's trance. She spun round to see who it was. She knew no one here. Only ghosts. This was no ghost however. On the contrary, the figure was solid, dressed in a sombre suit, a bowler hat set jauntily upon his head, the buttons of his waistcoat straining across his stomach. He was clean shaven, round-faced and beaming.

The shadow of a memory shimmered in her brain. The two of them, leaning up against the kitchen wall, smoking a cigarette, sharing a joke, casually flirting. Unable to find her voice, Vonny pointed vaguely in the direction of the Bursar's office, where she'd been sent to find somebody called Marge, who was her team leader.

He studied her for a long time before he finally spoke.

'So it is you,' was all he said.

Vonny decided to brazen it out. 'Well, it was last time I looked,' she said.

'Housekeeping said they was getting a bunch of new scouts. They didn't say you was one of them.'

She had a sudden glimpse of herself through his eyes. A forty-year-old woman, dressed in a nylon overall that crackled when she walked and cheap sandals, precariously held together by a couple of frayed straps. So she'd been right when she thought she caught him looking at her earlier, despite praying she was just another anonymous face in among the cluster of other women all reporting their arrival at the Porter's Lodge.

'I'd better get on,' she said.

But he wasn't quite ready to let her go yet, it seemed.

'I saw you earlier,' he said. 'But I was on the phone. When you left I looked you up on the list of new scouts just now. Vonny Quinn.'

'Quite the detective,' she said.

He smiled.

'You got sent down, didn't you? After that other business.'

That other business? Well, that was one way of describing it.

'You got me bang to rights, Guvnor,' she said, in a desperate bid to make light of things.

'What was it you did? To end up rusticated? There were all sorts of rumours.'

'Rumour is a pipe, blown by surmises, jealousies and conjectures,' she replied.

'Who said that? Shakespeare?'

'Henry the Fourth, Part One.'

She grinned. When he returned her grin, she caught a glimpse of the good-looking boy he'd once been, before time had wrapped the extra weight around his middle and his jaw.

'So you're the college porter now, then,' she said, before he could ask any more questions. 'I remember when you used to come round to New House and do the odd jobs. Always trying to cadge a cigarette you were.'

'As I remember it was the other way round,' he said.

She laughed. Her memory was fuzzy, she said.

'Is that your way of telling me to mind my own business about why you got sent down?'

He'd not forgotten then.

'Let's just say I never fitted in here from the start,' she said.

'Not everyone does,' he agreed. 'So, what, are you married? Kids? What you been doing all these years?'

'Perry,' she said. 'I've got a job to do. Twenty years is a lot to sum up in five minutes.'

'He gave her a mock salute. You're right,' he said. 'We'll catch up another time.'

Picking up her bucket she said something flippant about how she'd better get on if she didn't want to get fired before she even started.

'Maybe I'll run into you again,' she said, as, with a cheery wave she reluctantly began to move in the direction of New House. Funny, all these years had passed, yet this path was as familiar to her as the two-step walk from her bedroom at home in Assenden to the tiny bathroom she shared with Eddie. She pushed all thoughts of Eddie to the back of her mind. Just now she had enough to cope with.

'If Marge says anything to you about running late, just blame me.'

Perry's words carried back to her on the breeze. She gave another casual wave. Time was moving on and she'd loitered long enough. It was time to face her fears.

★   ★   ★

Naomi Sharp glanced at her phone to check the time and to see if there were any more messages from Kathy. It was well past eight now. She should have been here an hour ago. But that's what you got when you dated a police officer. Unreliability.

She'd chosen the window seat in the bar of the Lamb and Flag for a specific reason. She'd wanted to see Kathy's approach, so that she'd be ready for her when she came through the pub door. She'd already practised her acting face in the mirror in the lady's loo. Drooping shoulders and mouth, sad eyes to match. She'd managed to hold the expression for all of fifteen seconds. But then she'd caught sight of her reflection. That's when it became impossible to suppress her ecstatic grin. She'd never win an Oscar.

Although she'd waited for Kathy's arrival for so long now that she no longer felt like playing silly games. Perhaps she should just the text the news that she'd got the damn job instead and that if Kathy was still tied up at work then maybe they should forget about celebrating till the weekend, when both of them would be free.

Maybe they could go for a nice long walk on Sunday. Somewhere where the air was clean and where the pubs were a bit quieter than this one and served better food. The build-up to her interview had started one of her heads. It had got a bit better, briefly, after they'd called her back inside to say the job was hers. But now, a mix of blaring music and screeching people had ramped it right back up to barely tolerable.

She was just musing about how, when you didn't drink yourself you didn't appreciate the bonhomie so much, when her phone pinged into life again. It was another message from Kathy. When the first word was 'Sorry' was there any reason to read on, Naomi wondered.

When she did anyway she saw it was as she'd guessed. There was no way she was going to make it tonight.

'Did you hear about the SOCO job yet?' she'd added.

Before Naomi could text back a reply, the sound of raised voices coming from a table by the door leading to the courtyard made her turn her head. She'd glimpsed both parties before. Call it her police training but she only needed to see a face once and she never forgot it. She had the kind of tidy mind that had — apparently — made her the perfect candidate for the civilian job she'd swapped for her job as police constable — thanks to that stupid accident of hers that meant she was no longer fit for active service.

The woman, dark-haired, skinny and casually dressed in jeans and a jacket Naomi had heard Kathy describe as 'pleather', had been drinking on her own at a table in front of the massive flat screen TV when Naomi had first arrived. She'd been half way down the first glass from a bottle of white, her narrow jaw set in a way that suggested she was there till she'd finished the bottle's entire contents.

Naomi guessed she must have succeeded by now and would have been out the door already, had her attention not been caught by the solitary guy seated by the door, drinking his pint and minding his own business. Naomi had him down as a university type. A professor, probably. Senior lecturer at least. She'd often insisted to Kathy that you could spot them at a hundred paces. They always had a book with them, for one thing.

She couldn't make out what the woman was saying but her body language was aggressive. The man shrank back as she leaned towards him and repeatedly jabbed her finger in his face. That was another way you could tell the university types. They were unfailingly polite, even when being confronted by someone clearly spoiling for a fight.

The woman had obviously had far too much to drink. And there was an empty glass on the table dead handy for grinding his face into if he said anything to provoke her. Though so far, he'd said nothing at all.

Not that silence couldn't be provoking. On the contrary, there was nothing more infuriating than a man who failed to engage with a woman who wanted a row. And if a row was all it was, well, then maybe she should stay out of it even though she longed to intervene. She wasn't a police officer any more, she reminded herself. In her new role as scene of crime officer, she was a mere civilian.

It was as this thought popped into her head that the woman grabbed the man's glass and poured the contents over his head. Naomi watched, aghast, as it washed over his head and slid down his cheeks. The display was greeted by a mixed reception of cheers, applause and gasps from a nearby bunch of students, who, like Naomi, had observed the whole thing.

'Oh my,' she murmured as the woman, her task now complete, pushed open the door and left — somewhat unsteadily, it had to be said.

The man's reaction was muted. He inclined his head in the direction of his biggest audience — the group of students. The shadow of a smile flitted across his lips. Within moments, a rather pretty young girl was by his side. She handed him a couple of tissues with which he dabbed himself discreetly.

He was going to be all right, Naomi decided. And as a firm supporter of female solidarity she decided he must have done something to deserve such treatment. There was no smoke without fire, etcetera.

But what of the woman? It was dark outside now and she was drunk. Oxford was as safe as any other city in the UK if the statistics were to be believed. But if you didn't have your wits about you — and a bottle of white wine was bound to have stripped even the most seasoned drinker of a few of those — then that made you fair game for any predator chancing his luck with any lone woman unfortunate enough to cross his path.

Her very last case in fact, before she'd finally given in to pressure from Kathy and her boss and gone for the SOCO job, had been an assault on an Oxford woman walking through the park alone on her way home from a friend's leaving do. They'd never got the creep who did it, which suggested he was still at large.

It was an uneasy Naomi who shrugged on her jacket and made her way outside, deliberately avoiding meeting the gaze of the man who'd just been given the beer shampoo. Not that he'd have noticed her anyway. He was far too involved in a conversation with the pretty young woman who'd handed him the tissues. He had good taste, she'd give him that.

★　★　★

Vonny's triumphant exit from the pub didn't last long. She immediately took a wrong turning and was now totally confused about where the bus station was from here. She wandered along the pavement, occasionally glancing up at the now unfamiliar street names. It occurred to her, as she dodged the scaffolding outside a crooked row of shops, that the whole of Oxford city centre was in the process of being renovated.

When the strap of one of her sandals snapped, tripping her up inelegantly, to the unconcealed delight of a group of young Japanese tourists who happened to be passing by, she felt tears brimming. Today had been a pig of a day and she wasn't sure how much more she could take.

Spotting a doorway down a side street conveniently situated under a street light, she sat down, removed the offending sandal and began to dig inside her bag. Maybe there was something she could do to fix the damn thing for long enough to get her to the bus at least. But even as she rummaged, she knew the idea was hopeless. She'd never been the kind of woman to carry a sewing kit around with her. And even if she was and she'd had the right kind of needle, she'd had far too much to drink to be able to thread it.

Of all the bars in all the world she had to fetch up in the one Russ Pierson frequented. She'd gone there to drown her sorrows. Just a small glass of wine before she got on the bus that would drop her off home twenty minutes later. But then the barman had suggested she might as well buy a bottle as bottles were going for the same price as two glasses at the moment. She thought of the empty house she'd be going home to. Why not, she said. She'd drink a glass here and take the rest back with her.

But even while she handed over the money, carefully counting out every last penny, she knew that the chances of her doing that were as remote as Eddie ringing her up from Germany and telling her the band would have to find themselves another roadie because he missed her too much to stay another day.

Her anxiety had been mounting all day. This kind of job — foisted on her by the Job Centre, who'd threatened to stop her benefits if she turned it down — left a lot of time for thinking. Stripping beds and scrubbing toilets, emptying people's rubbish bins and carrying laundry up and down stairs might be onerous on the body, but it was hardly taxing on the mind.

Had this been a different hall, she might have coped better. Maybe even a different floor in New House. But she'd drawn the short straw. Thanks to Perry, who'd kept her talking and made her late, Marge had obviously got it in for her. New House, top floor, no arguments.

Nothing much had changed in the intervening years since she'd left. The rooms were as Spartan as ever. How many generations of students must have felt as irritated as she'd done to discover that the socket for her hairdryer was too far away to reach the mirror? Back then she'd been obsessed with her hair. It had to be big. That first time she'd washed it, ready for the fresher's ball, she'd left the door open and Phoebe had passed on her way downstairs, ethereal in her grey silk dress.

She must have heard Vonny swearing and wondered if she could help. That was the beginning of their friendship. How could she have failed to be reminded of the one single year she'd spent there and how dreadfully and abruptly it had ended?

One notable change had occurred since her time on the sixth floor in Room Ten, however. They'd fixed the window. These days, you could only open them so far and no further before they locked.

'Hey.'

Vonny craned her neck to see who it was standing in front of her. Reflected in the light of the street lamp she saw a woman about her own age, stocky, short hair with an orange streak running through it.

'Are you ok?' the stranger said.

She looked and sounded as if she really cared. It was just too much for Vonny right now. All day she'd been fighting back her emotions, doing the work of two women so as not to allow herself to feel anything. In fact, Marge had warned her more than once that if she carried on at that pace she wouldn't make many new friends among the other Scouts. Even then she'd found it hard to slow down.

The tears that all day had been gathering behind her eyes finally began to spill out, splashing onto the broken sandal she was still holding. In the distance a clock chimed the hour. How on earth could it be nine o'clock already?

'Dammit. There won't be another bus

now till ten. And I've got to be back here in the morning at eight on the dot.' She wafted her sandal about a few times. 'I guess this is how Cinderella must have felt,' she added, mournfully.

The woman grinned. 'So where are you going?' she said.

'Assenden. It's about twenty minutes away on the X5. Not even a village really. Not any more.'

'I know it,' the woman said. 'My car's just over there.' She pointed in the direction of the multi-storey. 'I can give you a lift if you like. It's not too far for you to hop.'

'I wouldn't want to put you out,' Vonny said.

'You wouldn't be. I've been stood up. And anyway I'm heading that way myself. Milton Keynes.'

'Well, in that case, yes please.' Vonny struggled to her feet. 'I'm Vonny, by the way,' she said.

'Naomi.'

They shook hands.

'Tell me something, Vonny, before we get in the car.' Naomi fixed Vonny with the kind of look it was going to be impossible to wriggle out from under. 'That guy back there. What was he? An ex or something?'

Vonny shook her head.

'No. Not an ex. I wasn't well-connected enough for him. He only liked posh girls.'

'So you were getting revenge for somebody else then?'

She was a smart one, no doubt about it, Vonny mused.

'It would take more than half a pint of beer to get revenge for what he did to Phoebe,' she said.

They'd reached the pelican crossing now. They waited at the edge of the pavement for the green man to give his permission to cross.

'Sounds bad,' said Naomi.

The green man began to bleep.

'It was bad, all right,' Vonny said. 'Russ Pierson was the man who killed my best friend.'

2

Last night, when Vonny had made the astonishing claim that Russ Pierson was responsible for the death of her best friend, Naomi had been taken aback, to say the least. She'd wanted to pry further but Vonny had clamped down immediately. She didn't want to talk about it, she said. She just needed to get home and go to bed.

So Naomi had driven her back to Assenden, where she said she lived. Vonny had fallen asleep almost as soon as they'd pulled out of the car park and she hadn't woken up till Naomi had shaken her awake on reaching their destination.

She'd dropped her off outside a tiny terraced house down a long badly-lit lane. Whereupon her passenger, still half-asleep and very possibly half-drunk as well, had stumbled out of the car, mumbling an embarrassed thank you. Naomi had waited till Vonny let herself safely inside and switched on some lights, then she'd driven off, hoping Vonny's hangover wouldn't stop her getting back into work the following day.

That should have been the end of that. Except it wasn't. She couldn't rid herself of the memory of Vonny tipping that beer over the head of the man she later described as the one who'd killed her best friend.

Russ Pierson, she'd said his name was. Back home, she googled him. There was a ton of information online. None of it made much sense to Naomi, since it concerned itself with the numerous papers he'd published in various august periodicals she'd never heard of. He was also the author of several volumes of non-fiction, all bearing the kind of esoteric titles that held no appeal to someone whose favourite author was Lee Child.

He was a fellow of St Rita's and had taught at Oxford University since 1995, receiving tenure there some five years later. He was married, so Google said, to a fellow academic. It was his second marriage.

Perhaps Vonny Quinn was simply a

fruit-loop. An alcoholic fruit-loop at that. She really ought to put the whole case behind her, Naomi thought, as she closed her laptop with a yawn. But she was intrigued by Vonny's claims. Her new job didn't start for at least another fortnight and Kathy was working all hours on the sex offence case. She needed a project. Digging up a bit of history on an old case that had long since been put to bed would do very nicely.

Next day she decided to do a bit more digging. Officially she was no longer a police officer. But she was still a familiar face around the nick. It wouldn't be seen as odd if she turned up out of the blue.

On her way in she waved nonchalantly to a couple of colleagues before taking a seat at the nearest available computer, all the while praying she wouldn't be accused of being an imposter. She was in luck. No one had got round to cancelling her password yet. Talk about a schoolboy error she thought, with an inward chuckle.

Since Vonny hadn't got round to giving her the name of her best friend, Naomi had been unable to find out anything about her when she'd been looking for stuff about Pierson. She hadn't said how long ago her friend's death had occurred either. But Naomi took a gamble on the fact that the two women had been friends — either as undergraduates or in some other capacity — roundabout twenty years previously, given the age Vonny looked now.

How many female suicides at St Rita's could there possibly have been over the course of the last twenty years anyway? To be on the safe side, she searched five years either side of her estimated guess. Even checking back over thirty years the answer came back to her as just one. Phoebe Flyte.

Her foray into the newspaper archives of the local paper gave the date of Phoebe Flyte's death — or rather the discovery of her body on the lawn at the foot of St Rita's College — as Tuesday 13th May, 1997. Photographs of her revealed her to have been pretty, petite and blonde.

Had she been plain and dumpy, Naomi doubted she'd have attracted half as much coverage as she had. Here was

Phoebe at her sister's wedding, sweetly attired in a simple bridesmaid's dress. There she was on the lawn of her family home, smiling prettily at the photographer. From the many snaps the paper had printed, it was impossible to tell anything about the kind of girls she was. Beyond her photo-ready smile she was giving nothing away.

Some of the comments by 'friends' of Phoebe had described her as 'fragile', 'lacking in self-confidence', 'the kind of girl who needed a prop if she was out for the night.' That prop being alcohol for the most part, though drugs were mentioned too. Also mentioned was her background, which explained the size of her back garden. It was massive.

Her father was a circuit judge and her mother was a surgeon at the Radcliffe, Naomi discovered. She was, apparently, the middle one of three, stuck between another doctor and an aspiring barrister. To say she came from a family of high-flyers was, perhaps, an understatement.

Once she'd learned all she could about

Phoebe's life, it was time to move on to her death. It was a small matter to access the coroner's report. She'd died, apparently, in the early hours of Tuesday May 13th 1997, after falling from the window of her room on the sixth floor of New House, St Rita's College, Oxford.

The medical cause of her death was described as a 'subdural and intracerebral haemorrhage' as a result of the fall. Traces of drugs and alcohol had been found in her body. According to the senior coroner, a Mrs Eleanor Marcus, Miss Flyte had had long-standing mental health issues, although none of these were specified in the report. It appeared to be a simple question of 'Death by misadventure while the balance of her mind was disturbed.'

So, if the verdict of misadventure had seemed so straightforward to the coroner, what had caused Vonny Quinn to think otherwise? This was where it started to get interesting. Leaning forward, Naomi began to read Vonny's statement. When she got to the end she switched off the computer, rose from her desk and hurried out of the building, a satisfied smile on her face and her mind working overtime,

They said, didn't they, that you could take the girl out of the job but you couldn't take the job out of the girl. Something like that, anyway, Naomi mused, as she fired up the engine of her little car. The statement Vonny had given to the coroner seemed to fly in the face of every other statement given by various members of her family, her tutors and her GP. Fine, there were more of them than there were of Vonny. But did that necessarily make them right and her wrong?

What she would have liked more than anything was to have another chat with Vonny Quinn. She knew where she worked and she knew where she lived too. But she couldn't just turn up without an excuse. Probably due to the wine she'd already said too much and knew she had. If she suspected Naomi was fishing for more titbits, she was pretty sure Vonny would send her packing with a flea in her ear.

There were road works ahead and a queue of vehicles in front of her that suggested she'd be stuck here forever.

Naomi began to tap the wheel with irritation. One of these days, when her legs felt stronger, she'd get back on her bike. There'd be none of this tedious time-wasting at the wheel then.

She leaned forward to grab the packet of mints she knew must be hiding somewhere in the glove compartment. And that's when her eyes fell on something sparkling on the floor by the passenger side, lit up by the sudden appearance of the sun's rays. It was a necklace. A small silver disc suspended by a silver chain.

Naomi caught her breath. She didn't recognise it as belonging to Kathy. Kathy's tastes were bigger and far bolder than this delicate little trinket. So that meant it could only belong to the last person she'd had in her car. Looked like fate had dropped the perfect excuse for her to pay Vonny a second visit right into her lap.

★ ★ ★

For a full twenty seconds after the alarm on her phone had woken Vonny from a deep sleep, the only thought in her head was coffee. But as she lay there a little longer, her gradually-awakening consciousness began to process other thoughts.

What was it she'd done last night? Her raging thirst and pounding head suggested alcohol had been involved. She was about to call out for Eddie, to see if he could jog her memory, then she remembered.

Eddie and she had split up. Or they may as well have. Now he was on a three-month trip with some ageing rock band on a tour of Northern Europe, acting as their roadie. He didn't want to go, he'd said. But what choice did he have in the end? It was a remark that had been his constant cry right up until the moment he said his final goodbye two nights previously.

They were at the door, waiting for the van to pick him up.

'This isn't what I want, Vonny. But you've left me no choice,' he'd said, hitching his rucksack onto his back.

She was fighting a huge lump in her throat at the sight of him. Despite the beard and the tattoos and the kind of physique that meant other guys only ever looked at him with respect in their eyes, Eddie had a certain vulnerability about him that made him no threat to women.

She was fighting something else too. Her own obstinacy and downright pig-headedness. She'd been fighting it ever since she'd first got to know him.

'You don't want to know about my past,' she'd said, when he got to prying a bit too closely about her life before she'd known him.

She'd fed him scraps to keep him quiet. He knew she'd been to university. She'd told him Newcastle for some crazy reason she could barely remember now. Lying was a habit when it hurt too much to speak the truth.

He knew she'd left after a year too. Her mother, who'd since died, had been ill, she'd told him, and there was no one else to take care of her. She guessed he believed her because he'd dropped the subject ages ago.

When she'd semi-woken that first time, in the middle of the night, screaming and gasping for breath, he'd coaxed her back to full awakening. It was just a nightmare, she said. Talk to me, he said, tell me what it was about. But she refused and still refused each subsequent time it woke her, always insisting it was nothing.

How would it ever have helped to tell him about the rush of air, the falling body, the splintering of bones and that last, final thud that had broken Phoebe's neck as she met the ground below? People said that if you spoke about your bad dreams they never troubled you again. But for Vonny, speaking about that night was more than she could bear. She preferred to keep it buried.

Except she should have known that the thing you thought you'd buried was bound to to claw its way back up sooner or later. And it had. The last time she went to sign on they told her they had a job for her as a cleaner at her St Rita's. She'd come back in a filthy mood. Yelled at Eddie for forgetting to empty the dishwasher and eating the last banana. Barely spoken to him over dinner.

'Why won't you talk to me properly about this? Tell me why you don't want to take this job at St Rita's?' he asked her.

She'd given him the same reason she'd given him for turning down all the other jobs in Oxford they'd previously offered her.

'Oxford's too far to go on the bus and back every day,' was how she'd explained her refusal. 'The buses are rubbish and I'd end up paying most of what I earned on transport.'

Besides, didn't she do enough cleaning here at home? She hoped, given she had right on her side with this, since Eddie had to be the messiest person she'd ever had to share a space with, that he'd leave her alone after that. But it wasn't to be.

'If we both moved to Oxford then we could both get work there. You could get bar work. I'd come and pick you up if you had to work late.'

'I don't want to move to Oxford. And that's an end of it.'

What was wrong with Oxford, he wanted to know. Everything, she snapped back. It was big, it was dirty, it was full of tourists and anyway she liked it where she was. Except there were no jobs here, Eddie reminded her.

'The trouble with you is that you refuse to make compromises,' he'd snapped.

'That's not true,' she retorted. 'I told the woman at the Job Centre I'd take either of the other jobs she'd offered me before this one.'

'Oh. You mean those other jobs you turned down because they happened to be in Oxford too?'

His voice dripped sarcasm.

'Yes.'

'And what did she say?'

'That they'd already been snapped up.'

'You do know you'll be sanctioned if you don't take this one, don't you,' Eddie said, quietly.

There was no need to rub her nose in it, she said. She was perfectly well aware of the rules. The very next day she'd rung up the Job Centre and accepted the Scout's job. But later, when she let him know and Eddie moved towards her to try to take her in his arms and make up their quarrel, she'd backed away. She wasn't doing it for him, she said. She was doing it because she had no choice. The day after that was the day he made the call to one of his old mates from back in the day and landed the roadie job.

Vonny reached for her phone to check if he'd texted her. Her heart leapt when she saw she had a message. So he'd come out of his bad mood. He still loved her and he was texting her to tell her so.

But when she opened it she realised it wasn't from Eddie at all. It was from Perry. What on earth was he doing texting her when he could speak to her at work, she mused, quashing her disappointment?

Unless. Her stomach did a nose dive. Russ Pierson. My God! How could she have forgotten what had happened last night? She sat up in bed and covered her eyes with her hands. But it was impossible to block out the memory of the incident in the pub. As if on a loop the scene played out in her mind over and over again. She felt sick.

What if Perry were texting her to tell her Pierson had lodged an official complaint and that as of this moment she was sacked? How on earth was she going to explain this mess to Eddie? Maybe she wouldn't need to, if Eddie kept up his silence. Maybe he'd already put her right behind him and was even now lying in the arms of some German Fraülein he'd picked up after last night's gig?

She skim-read Perry's message. When she registered that there was no mention of Pierson's name anywhere in his text she read it again, this time more slowly.

'Help!' he'd written. 'We're having a crisis. There's a conference on this weekend and we're desperate for staff. It's a late finish both nights but pay's good and there's accommodation for those who live too far from college to travel back home. Please say you'll do it.'

Vonny thought about it for precisely five seconds. What did she have to lose? She needed the money, that was for sure. And she'd only be wasting her time if she spent the weekend at home waiting for Eddie to ring her. But what about Pierson? Her finger hovered over the keys while she thought about the possibility of him seeking her out, plotting how to get his own back for what she'd done to his precious ego last night in that bar.

She'd call the Porter's Lodge and tell

Perry she'd do the extra hours. And as for Russ Pierson. He could go hang.

★ ★ ★

Vonny didn't think she'd be able to get through it. She hadn't stopped since she'd got here, making up beds for the conference guests then dashing over to housekeeping to get her instructions for where to be to serve coffee, which, she soon learned, was to be served in the marquee.

The rest of the day had followed in a whirl. Lunch, then afternoon tea, drinks and dinner. She'd barely had a minute to herself all weekend, but she'd been glad of it. It meant there was no time to dwell on Eddie or to think about Russ Pierson and what he might have in mind for her, if anything at all.

As Saturday drew to a close, she was daring to think she'd got away with it. For a start, Pierson appeared to have been off campus, which was a huge relief. Secondly, she'd picked up no signal from Perry that she was in trouble with the powers-that-be. In fact, he'd been full of praise for the way she was mucking in.

She reminded him that as a student she'd worked silver service during the vacation to make some money to get her through the rest of the term.

'Once you've got it you never lose it,' she'd joked, briefly pausing to exchange a few words with him in the middle of serving dinner.

Today, Sunday, hadn't been without some unease, however. Russ Pierson was back in the dining room at lunchtime. Several times she'd been aware of him watching her. She'd done her best to avoid him and for the most part it had worked.

But this evening, at drinks, he'd taken a glass of champagne from the tray she'd been proffering at the entrance to the marquee. She'd held her breath as he'd taken the glass from her and refused to meet his eye.

'Am I safe?' he drawled, in that cultured, overly-confident voice of his. 'Or should I expect another glass over my head?'

It would have been easy to make some clever-clever reply. It would have been a waste of a good vintage, for example. But she'd remained tight-lipped. Tomorrow she'd be back on bed-making duties in New House and needn't have anything more to do with him, she thought, as she crossed the quad and came out onto the path that led to Garden House, where she'd been allocated a tiny box room on the ground floor for the duration of her stay.

It was dark in the grounds but for a few lights in the windows. Vonny picked her way along the uneven path. The scent of roses from the bushes that lined her route was a welcome alternative to the odour of stale food which clung to her clothes.

She was just thinking what a relief it would be to get out of them when she caught a sound from somewhere deep within the bushes. At first it was simply a rustle of foliage, but then there came a crackle of twigs followed by the ragged sound of breathing. Vonny froze, gripped by a strong sense that she was not alone. Someone was in hiding, observing her, waiting for the right moment to pounce.

She held her breath, aware of her heart racing. She longed to speak, to challenge whoever it was who was lying in wait for her. But she was too terrified. She stared in horror as the rose bush started to shake violently before it parted to reveal the dark shape of someone crouching, ready to pounce.

3

Her first thought was that Russ Pierson was lying in wait for her. The fact that he'd kept his distance all day was obviously a clever ruse to woo her into a false state of security. But now, standing alone under the blue-black sky of an early autumn night, he was about to get his own back for the other night and what she'd done to him.

She waited, stiff with fear but on her guard, ready to defend herself, if need be. But then she remembered that Russ was bigger than her, stronger than her and, worse, she'd humiliated him and he was angry. Russ Pierson was a man you humiliated at your peril. She'd already discovered that before.

When the bushes parted it took her a while to compute that this fuzzy outline of a pair of upright ears and horns that resembled two stiff scallops was no human but an animal. The creature dipped its head then raised it again, briefly holding her gaze.

She held her breath, waiting for it to spring but after its initial curiosity it seemed to have lost interest in her. She followed its movements as, with one bound it shot past her across the lawn. The last thing she saw — thanks to the old gas lamps that shed a dim yellow light along the route of the main path — was its illuminated white behind disappearing into the darkness.

Vonny threw back her head and began to roar with laughter. A muntjac. She should have guessed. Those damn deer where everywhere round these parts, munching the roses, barking through the night, scaring the living daylights out of innocent passers-by.

The first time she'd encountered one had been back in her student days. Apparently, so someone told her, some famous landowner had brought a couple over from China for his private zoo. But they'd escaped and begun to breed copiously. Now they ran wild throughout Oxfordshire and for all she knew had migrated to other parts of the country too.

It was with a much lighter step that Vonny finally reached her destination. She was tired but was still determined to grab that shower. When she crawled into bed at close to midnight she hadn't anticipated any trouble sleeping.

But her current situation made a restful sleep impossible. The bed was narrow and the mattress was thin. The smallest movement she made set off a series of creaks. Twenty years had passed since she'd spent a night in student halls. But it was as if she'd never been away. With every door that clanged shut along the corridor and with each rattle of the ancient heating system, she was catapulted back to those days when, as an undergraduate, she'd stuff earplugs in her ears and sleep with a pillow over her head to shut out the noise.

Hours passed, it seemed to her, before she eventually fell asleep. But no sooner had she done so than she was awake again. For the first time in months, she'd had that dream. Phoebe falling, floating, to the ground. She'd fought her way back to consciousness, wrenching open her eyes just in time to avoid the ugly crunch of her body hitting the ground. For the second time that night her thudding heart went in overdrive.

She lay there, waiting for the night to settle round her again, grateful for the orchestrated percussion of slamming doors and rumbling radiators. But beyond those sounds there came another. Someone was turning the handle of her door. Once. Twice. Three times.

'Hello?' she cried out, struggling to keep her voice firm. 'Who's there?'

She held her breath but there was nothing. Just silence. She switched on her lamp and crept silently out of bed, padding across the floor on bare feet to try the door for herself. She was almost certain she'd locked it — it was a reflex action that anyone who'd ever lived communally never forgot. But maybe tonight she'd forgotten, thrown off balance by exhaustion and her encounter with the muntjac.

She took a deep breath, thrust out her hand and pulled down hard on the handle. If it had opened and she'd come face to face with whoever was on the other side, she had no idea how she'd have responded. Luckily she didn't have to. Exactly as she'd prayed it would, the door refused to budge.

Russ Pierson. It had to be him. She'd been foolish to think she'd escaped his wrath totally. He was waiting for her. And it was only a matter of time before he caught up with her.

* * *

Perry was outside New House, leaning against a wall and smoking a cigarette as she struggled up the path, her arms full of bedding. Was he waiting for her? Memories of last night's events still haunted her. Was it because she'd refused to open up to let Russ into her room that Perry was here now? To tell her a complaint had been made against her and she'd been fired? When he saw her, he dropped his cigarette end and ground it beneath his heel.

'Here, let me take that,' he said. 'You're

not looking too clever this morning.'

It never came naturally to Vonny to accept a man's help — probably one more reason why Eddie, to whom chivalry came so naturally, had decided that the two of them were never really going to hit it off together long term.

But after her sleepless night she had no fight left in her. Or rather, the bit of fight she still had, she was saving till she saw Russ Pierson again. Last night, newly woken, lying in the dark, barely knowing where she was, she'd been afraid. But in broad daylight she felt differently. She'd never been a woman to go quietly. And if there was anyone who understood that then it should be Pierson.

'Thanks,' she said. Then, as he took the load from her she added, 'Did you want me for something?'

She spoke with confidence, but dreaded his reply. Perry's hand went to his inside pocket. She was certain he was about to hand her her P45.

'Someone dropped this off at the Porter's Lodge.' He handed her a rather crumpled white envelope.

'Did they leave a name?'

She took the envelope from him and tested the contents with her fingers. It felt like it contained nothing at all.

'Some woman,' he said. 'Short. Orange streak in her hair. Bit of a limp.'

The woman called Naomi. Did she fancy Vonny or something? Vonny really ought to have put her straight that she didn't bat for the same team, before she'd got out of her car last night. Especially since this morning, she'd found Naomi's card in her bag.

'Oh. Okay.'

'You sound relieved. Were you expecting bad news?'

'Not really,' she lied.

She thrust the envelope into her overall pocket.

'Aren't you going to open it? See what it is?'

People never changed. Perry had always been the nosey type. She could have told him to mind his own business. But then she remembered just in time that in theory he was her superior.

'It'll wait,' she said, pressing the button

for the lift. 'Thanks, Perry,' she added, when it became apparent he was still hanging around.

'You've got the top floor then,' he said.

The lift was on its way down already. Vonny picked up her laundry load.

'Does it bother you still? Because if it does, I can always ask Marge to have a word with housekeeping. See if they'll change the rota.'

He looked genuinely concerned. So much so that it was all she could do not to choke on the lump in her throat that was growing bigger by the second. It was a relief when the lift arrived and the doors slid open. Vonny stepped inside.

'No need for that, Perry,' she said, plastering her face with a bright smile.

'Well, you know where to find me if you feel like a chat.'

She nodded her head enthusiastically and said she'd definitely drop in on him as soon as she got a chance. It was only when the doors closed and she found herself on her way up to the top floor, that she allowed her face to crumple.

★ ★ ★

Vonny fingered the chain around her neck, nervously. Eddie had given it to her on their six-month anniversary. She felt bad that she'd not even missed it till now. She felt worse when she remembered how she'd had a go at him for giving it to her in the first place.

Who remembers six-months, she'd said? It's not even a proper anniversary. Honestly, sometimes she could have bitten her own tongue off. She didn't deserve a man like Eddie. Not that she had him anymore, she reminded herself.

'I didn't think you'd feel like running into Russ Pierson again, after what you said,' Naomi said, stirring her coffee, before raising the cup to her lips. 'That's why I suggested this place.'

'This place' was a trendy, hipster coffee shop just round the corner from St Rita's.

'So it's not because you don't trust me round booze, then?'

Naomi laughed. 'Not at all,' she said.

'You had my address,' Vonny said. 'How come you didn't just stick it in the post?'

251

'I wanted to talk to you about what happened to your friend Phoebe,' said Naomi.

Vonny stiffened.

'Are you police?'

Naomi shook her head. She looked a touch sad, Vonny thought.

'Ex.' She tapped her leg with the hand that wasn't holding the coffee cup. 'Stupid cycling accident,' she said. 'Got mashed up by a car. I've had to retrain.'

'As a what?'

'A civilian job,' was all she would admit to.

'Well, you sound like police to me.' Vonny was suspicious by nature. 'All this wanting to speak to me. Asking questions.'

'I'm just nosy,' Naomi said. 'What you said the other night was pretty strong stuff, Vonny. You can't expect an ex-cop not to do a bit of digging around.'

Vonny leaned across the table. 'I was drunk. I was angry. Being back here at St Rita's brought back bad times,' she said. 'Phoebe's death was an accident. Everybody said so.'

'Everybody but you.'

Vonny shrugged and took a sip of her drink.

'So you've read my statement to the coroner, then?'

Naomi nodded. Shifting her gaze away from Naomi's piecing grey-blue eyes, Vonny tried concentrating on her coffee. It wasn't so easy.

'You said something just now,' Naomi said. 'Something about you being back at St Rita's.'

It hadn't escaped Vonny that Naomi had put the emphasis on the word 'back'. Suddenly Vonny longed for a cigarette.

'You're not giving up are you?' she snapped. 'If you must know, I was an undergrad at St Rita's. Read one year of English then left.'

That's all you're getting, mate, she thought. Though Naomi had already moved on.

'So you would have known Phoebe well.'

'We were best friends.'

'What about her parents? What did you know about them?'

Only what Phoebe told her about them, she replied, wondering why Naomi should have taken such a sudden interest in those two. They were clever, she said, like everyone in Phoebe's family.

'Although Phoebe always maintained that if she'd gone to my school and had my background she'd never even have got as far as GCSEs, let alone to Oxford.'

She'd never been envious when Phoebe had described how she'd grown up. Everyone her family knew was a somebody, Vonny explained. A curator in an art gallery; a Nobel scientist; some top lawyer who'd probably helped found the Geneva Convention or something.

'Round hers you were a failure if you had less than eight letters after your name,' she quipped.

Naomi smiled.

'So you'd have said it was important that they gave their daughter every opportunity in life?'

'Goes without saying.'

'Then why do you think they weren't as willing to give her the same chance in death?'

Vonny, who hitherto had been more engrossed in her coffee than in this conversation, suddenly grew interested.

'What do you mean?'

'They just accepted the coroner's verdict. That Phoebe committed suicide while the balance of her mind was disturbed,' Vonny said. 'Given what you told the Coroner — that she'd been in a bad place for a long time but that finally she'd come out of it and was looking forward to her mother's birthday drinks that night — why didn't they make more of a fuss?'

Vonny didn't reply.

'If that had been my daughter I'd have pursued it. From the evidence you gave, she had a purpose. Yet her parents just rolled over when the coroner pronounced suicide.'

Didn't she think it was odd, Naomi said.

Vonny drained her cup and stood up. She needed to get back to St Rita's, she said. They were short staffed and she'd got someone else's rooms to do as well as her own.

'And no,' she added. 'I don't think it's odd that they preferred the version offered up by trusted professionals, to my version.'

'You speak like you weren't to be trusted,' Naomi said.

'Put it this way. My background, the way I dressed and spoke. It hardly made me a reliable witness in their eyes.' Vonny snatched up her bag. 'Thanks for the coffee,' she said.

And then she was gone, out of the door and on to the street. That ex-copper thought herself so clever, sniffing around trying to find things out about Phoebe's family. But she knew nothing. Nothing at all.

★　★　★

'Very good of you to turn up.'

Marge was in the middle of unlocking the broom cupboard on the first floor landing of New House when Vonny showed up, out of breath from running most of the way from the café.

'Where do you want me?' Vonny

replied, ignoring the sarcasm.

'Main house. Top floor. Fellows' rooms.'

Vonny's stomach gave a back flip.

'Will they be empty now?' she said.

'I wouldn't send you if I knew there were people there now, would I?'

Marge obviously got her kicks from showing those below her who was boss. Vonny held her hand out for the keys. It was a slight victory to show absolutely no reaction at all to the woman's bullying manner.

Russ Pierson's room was the end one on the corridor. Curiosity sent her there first. When her sharp rap at the door was met with silence she let herself inside with a great deal of clatter and chinking of keys.

The room was large, the furnishings minimal. He was lucky, she thought, to nab not just the biggest room but also the one that had the sun on it all day. Lucky, or — more likely — just insistent.

She told herself she had no interest in looking at his things. She just wanted to get on and get out. But all the same her eyes were drawn to his possessions cluttering his desk and his books on the shelves and. She wandered over to them, running a finger along the spines as she glanced at the familiar names. Shakespeare was there of course, in abundance. And Milton too. Had she really ploughed through *Paradise Lost* during her time here?

Her eye was drawn to a slim paperback squashed between two sturdy hardbacks. It was Sylvia Plath's *The Bell Jar*. That had been Phoebe's favourite book. Just the sight of it squatting on Russ Pierson's bookshelf summoned Phoebe's presence before her. She could see her now, the first time she'd wandered into Vonny's room wearing that grey silk dress she'd picked up from a charity shop, wispy tendrils escaping from her upswept hair, and her thin shoulder blades protruding from the backless dress like the nubs of an angel's wings.

How different they'd been from each other, Phoebe and herself. Phoebe was the girl with the connections and the exquisite manners, the very opposite of

Vonny, who used to quip that she'd been dragged up, not brought up. Everything was wrong with her, she often used to think. She didn't know how proper conversation worked for one thing. Where she came from, people didn't take turns to speak. And they didn't always put a filter on their words either.

Before she properly got to know Phoebe — and later too, when Phoebe and she had fallen out — she spent a lot of time with Perry. They were two of a kind, he'd say and she'd agree. But even as the two of them shared cigarettes and poked fun at the posh kids with their talk of 'gap yahs' and ski-ing holidays, Vonny knew this wasn't true.

They may have shared the same background but that was where their similarities ended. Vonny loved books and learning and though she may have sneered at some of the other more privileged students, deep down she envied their confidence and the ease with which they appeared to her to drift through their days.

But despite that, she no more wanted to be like them than she wanted to be like

Perry. The truth was she didn't think she fitted in anywhere. And as the weeks went by during that first term, it suddenly began to dawn on her that maybe Phoebe's confidence was a mere trick and that, actually, she no more fitted in at Oxford than Vonny did.

In fact, she soon began to see that her new friend was terrified of life. She just had better coping strategies. Booze, of course. Well, every undergraduate knew about that. But then there were the pills. They helped her stay awake at night, so she could get through the pile of reading she was expected to do and write all the essays she was expected to write, was how she explained it to Vonny.

When the essays came back with poor marks and a request from her tutor to go and see him so they could talk about it, Vonny had done her best to reassure her. Nobody wanted her to fail, she insisted. The tutors were there to help.

When Phoebe returned from her meeting she'd given her a hug and thanked her. Vonny had been right, she said. Russ, her tutor, had offered to help her in any way he could to bring her marks up to scratch. And that had been the start of Phoebe and Russ's affair.

Had Vonny really been concerned about Phoebe's welfare or had she just been jealous of losing her best friend? A concerned person would have reported Pierson to the Vice Chancellor, for he was a man who was abusing his position of power over a vulnerable student.

But she didn't do that, did she? She simply stood by and watched it happen. Grew irritated when Phoebe began to preface every single conversation with the words, 'Russ said' or 'Russ thinks'. Interrupted her just when she'd got going about some deep discussion about Sylvia Plath she'd had with him. Ignored her pointedly when she came home late at night after she'd been — or so she said — studying late in Russ's room. And some nights, not returning to her own room at all.

Vonny tugged at the flimsy paperback, jammed between the other two sturdier volumes. A flimsy piece of paper floated from between the pages of the paperback onto the bed. A glance down at the page was enough to allow her to glimpse the words 'Darling Russ' and the final signature. Phoebe. The door handle rattled and turned. Something compelled her to snatch up the letter and shove it in her pocket.

And then a head appeared round the door.

'What the hell are you doing in my room?'

It was Russ Pierson. And this time there was no escape.

4

Russ Pierson gripped the door handle like he wished it were her neck. His face was livid. Vonny dropped the book she'd been holding and jumped up from the bed.

'What's your game, Vonny?'

Somehow she was going to have to get past him. But he was standing squarely in front of the door, blocking her way.

'Bit ironic, don't you think?' he sneered. 'Last time you broke into my room you took a hammer to my computer and destroyed the book I was working on back then.'

'I hope it taught you a valuable lesson about backing up your stuff,' she said.

It was the first thing she could think of. Pathetic, but it was going to have to do.

He rolled his eyes.

'Lived up to your expectations, has it, life on the minimum wage?' he sneered back.

She wanted to kill him.

'So much promise. Wasted.' He mimed

blowing out a candle. 'Pouf! All so you could get some sick revenge for some twisted idea that I killed Phoebe.'

'I need to leave now,' she said, refusing to engage with him any longer. 'I've got other rooms to do.'

'Well then don't let me stop you.'

Slowly and deliberately he stepped aside to allow her to pass. The space between them was so tight she could feel the static between them. Was this some new trick he was playing, allowing her to get so far before he reached out and grabbed her? Then what would he do? Kill her too, like he killed Phoebe?

She was at the door now, her body rigid, her breath controlled. She just needed to walk down the stairs and then she'd be outside. Safe. With every step she took, she half expected a hand on her shoulder, then a mighty shove. An accident, he'd say, that's all it was.

But Russ hadn't budged and she was only inches away from the first landing landing now. Two more steps and she was there. From the landing window she spotted Perry from the bowler hat he wore as part of his uniform. He was dragging a cart full of books behind him, probably on his way to the library. There were plenty of students about too, some walking alone glued to their phones, others in pairs or larger groups, engrossed in conversation.

The next flight of stairs she took at speed. Finally, she'd arrived at the outer door. Flinging it open she ran outside to embrace her freedom.

★ ★ ★

Kathy was working late again. There'd been another sex attack though she hadn't given the details since the investigation was top secret, she said. Though she had revealed that by going back in time through records they'd started to believe that this latest spate of attacks on women might have been linked with other attacks that had taken place a few years previously, for whom they'd never found a culprit.

Naomi sat back on the settee, hugging her mug of steaming tea. The TV was showing some nonsense she wasn't really watching, which was perhaps why her thoughts turned to Vonny. Was she still drinking alone in pubs, passing time before her bus back home arrived, she wondered?

She hated the idea of telling other women they should stay home, or, if they did venture out of the house, that they should get home well before it got dark. Women had as much right to be out on the town as men and if anybody needed to be given any advice, then it was men who attacked women, who needed to be told not to. And other women who judged them for daring to demand the same kind of freedom that men took for granted.

But all the same, just before she went to bed, she found herself dialing Vonny's number, just to hear her say that she was safe. All things considered, her reply was only what she ought to have expected.

★   ★   ★

'I thought I told you to leave me alone.'

This was the second time since she'd got home after her encounter with Russ that Vonny's phone had rung from an unknown number. The first time she'd snatched it up, hoping it might be Eddie, ringing her from some stranger's phone. In fact, it had been Perry, calling her from a college number to ask if she fancied doing another later night dinner shift at college the following night.

She'd been sharp with him. Two minutes into his chronicle of woe about the unreliability of temps she butted in. She was sorry if Perry had been inconvenienced, she said. But sorting out the staffing problems of St Rita's was one task that was way above her pay scale. It was too short notice and she couldn't do it.

As soon as she'd rung off she realised she'd probably gone too far. He was just doing his job. After all, she had informed the college when they'd hired her that she didn't mind being rung at home on the off chance she could help them out in an emergency.

She would have rung him back there and then and apologised. But that's when it rang again, putting an end to that idea. For the second time her heart had lifted when she hadn't recognised the number. And for the second time her hopes were dashed when she heard Naomi's voice, saying how she hoped Vonny didn't mind being called at home.

When she asked after her Vonny had snapped out her reply, then immediately hung up and thrown her phone across the room. Tears of self-pity sprang to her eyes. She was lonely, she was tired and her nerves were in shreds. So why on earth was she being so rotten to the two people who'd reached out to her in friendship? Was it surprising that Eddie had grabbed the first opportunity to flee the country in order to get away from her? Who needed a miserable old harridan as a girlfriend?

But she needed Eddie. If he were here she wouldn't have behaved so badly to Naomi and Perry. He was her better half and his kindness and generosity rubbed off on her whenever he was around.

Vonny dropped to her knees and crawled over to the corner of the room where her phone lurked in amongst the dust behind the TV. She dialled Eddie's number. It rang half a dozen times before it went to voice mail. It wasn't even his voice, she thought, ruefully. Just a collection of colourless, automatic syllables knitted together to tell her to leave a message. She took a deep breath and began.

'Eddie. It's me,' she said. 'I miss you. And I love you. I'm sorry for being a total cow most of the time. And I want you to come home.'

There. She'd said everything she needed to say. Anything else would have been superfluous. She ended the call and stared at the phone, willing it to start ringing. After a minute or more of this, she knew it wasn't going to. It was getting late. She needed to get ready for another early start in the morning.

Her dirty overall was hanging over a chair arm in the kitchen. If she put it through a quick wash it would be ready for morning. She quickly went through the pockets and retrieved a balled up tissue, a stick of chewing gum and a flimsy, folded piece of paper. It was the letter she'd found trapped between the pages of the book of Sylvia Plath's poetry on Pierson's bookshelf. With everything else that had been rushing through her mind she'd forgotten all about it.

She sat down on the one kitchen chair that didn't have at least one dodgy leg and carefully unfolded the paper, grown fragile over the years.

'Dear, sweet, clever, kind and generous Russ,' she read. 'Vonny always tells me that I have perfect manners. So, here you go — a thank you letter.'

Vonny smiled to see her name on the page, written in Phoebe's neat, round, schoolgirl handwriting. It was certainly true. When it came to matters of etiquette that girl had never put a foot wrong.

'I have a lot of things to thank you for, actually,' the letter continued. 'For mopping up my tears that first time I came to you and told you I was out of my depth. For holding my hand through all those essays and never losing patience when I got muddled. Most of all, for building up my self-confidence and for believing in me the way my family never did.

'I'm not like them. I never was. This academic life isn't for me. So I'm quitting uni. You said everyone has a talent. Well, maybe it's about time I ventured into the world and discovered mine. I'll leave the clever stuff to you and Von.

At the risk of repeating myself, thank you. You've been a good friend. Phoebe.'

Vonny read the letter again and again, through tears that grew increasingly blurred. It didn't make sense, the things Phoebe had written to Pierson. The things she'd written *about* him too. This letter had been written by a woman with her head held high. Finally, it seemed, she'd understood something about the world and about herself. And from what she'd just read, it looked like Russ Pierson had been the one to reveal it to her.

Could Vonny possibly have got him wrong? Had she just been jealous of Russ, because his influence over Phoebe had been stronger than her own? Vonny considered her twenty- year-old self. She thought she was so smart back then, compared to the silver-spooners, as she used to describe them. The privileged kids who might have had the grey matter but when it came to being streetwise had no idea.

But she'd been just as naïve as

everybody else, full of herself and her own ridiculous prejudices. It had suited her to see Pierson as a sleazebag whose main aim was to play Svengali to Phoebe's Trilby. But maybe he'd been her guru, not her seducer.

Her mind went back to the last time she and Phoebe had spoken. It was the night before she died. Vonny had had a message from Phoebe to meet her at the Union, in the bar. She remembered she hadn't wanted to go. She was still sulking for a start. And she hated the idea of being summoned, like Phoebe was Lady Muck and she was some impoverished lackey.

Six weeks previously they'd had a huge fall-out over Russ. Vonny had said some awful things, not just about Russ — Phoebe already knew what she thought of him and she'd heard it all before. But about Phoebe too.

Cruel, personal stuff. She'd accused her of being weak and feeble and the worst kind of feminist, who paid feminism lip-service by reading the right books and sporting the T-shirts with the right slogans but who was incapable of making a decision without deferring to a man.

Because they'd lived in the same house, on the same floor and attended the same lectures, it had been impossible to ignore each other. Weeks of avoiding each other followed. Whenever they did bump into each other Vonny simply blanked Phoebe.

That was when she started hanging out with Perry, because without Phoebe, frankly, she had no friends. Or none she wanted to hang out with for very long. Phoebe, on the other hand, not only had Russ, but a shoal of friends too. Not just from university but old school chums she'd grown up in Oxford with.

Was it loneliness, rather than the realisation that she'd overstepped the mark with Phoebe, that made her respond to Phoebe's note, slipped beneath her door one night, asking if they could meet the following evening?

Their meeting had been short and — on Vonny's part at least — awkward. She hadn't known what to expect. Would Phoebe throw herself at Vonny sobbing that she wished they'd never fallen out and saying how much she longed for them to be friends again?

Or had she come to show the girl from the council estate how to be civil by extending the hand of — if not exactly friendship — then courtesy for the rest of the academic year. After which the two of them would both be at liberty to find new lodgings away from halls and from each other?

What she got was neither. Phoebe seemed elated. Like someone hugging a secret. There was a new confidence about her. She couldn't stay, she said. It was her mother's birthday and she'd been summoned to raise a glass, along with the rest of her family.

Usually, when Phoebe spoke about her family, particularly about her mother, her shoulders drooped and her head hung low. But that very last night, after which Vonny would never see her friend alive again, Phoebe's manner was so serenely confident that Vonny couldn't help feel in awe of her. She watched Phoebe walk away, a spring in her step, a smile on her face and a nonchalant toss of her lovely hair as she turned to wave a final goodbye.

★ ★ ★

Vonny had relented. Next morning she'd turned up at work with her overnight bag and headed straight for the Porter's Lodge, where she caught Perry still in a flap because of his seemingly ongoing staffing problem.

'You're serious?' he'd said, when she told him she'd slept on it and decided she might as well help him out as stay at home and wait for a call from her boyfriend that would never come.

'And I'm sorry for being a bit short with you too,' she added, for good measure.

'Was you?' he said, po-faced. 'Can't say I noticed.'

It was just silly banter between work colleagues, but it lifted her spirits and got her through her busy morning. She'd barely smiled since Eddie had gone off to Germany. And actually, she hadn't had much to smile about in the run up to him going, either.

Once en route to New House for her cleaning shift, she made a decision that she wasn't going to think about Eddie for the rest of the day and in that spirit she turned off her phone. If he chose today to ring her for the first time, then he'd get a taste of what he'd been giving her for the past week. Total silence.

She zipped through her morning's work with a vigour she hadn't felt in a long time. Only occasionally did she allow herself to think about Phoebe's letter and any new thoughts that crept into her head about Russ, she immediately blocked. It was just too confusing to see him in any other light other than the one she'd been viewing him for the last twenty years.

So she thought she was ready for him when he approached her out of nowhere as she was clearing glasses after dinner from the reception area in the Old Hall.

'I think you've got something of mine,' he said, marching up to her, his academic gown flying behind him.

Vonny stiffened. 'I have no idea what you're talking about,' she said, defensively.

He came to a halt in front of her, boxing her into a corner.

'You were in my room yesterday looking through my things and . . . '

'No. No I wasn't.'

'Don't lie to me.'

'I'm not lying. Yes, I was in your room. But I was there to clean it and that was all I did.'

Any softening she'd been beginning to feel towards the man who now towered above her immediately melted. Who the hell did he think he was, accosting her like this? He didn't deserve her pity or her understanding. The only thing Russ Pierson deserved was her contempt.

'What's going on here?'

The squeak of Perry's shiny black shoes alerted her to his arrival even before his voice. She sent him a glance of gratitude as he came striding towards them. Russ Pierson was the big man when it came to a one to one confrontation. But he had his reputation to think of within college. He wasn't going to risk it by taking on the college porter. Perry's position conferred almost as much clout as he'd have received had he been Vice-Chancellor.

'Nothing.'

Vonny and Pierson spoke the word simultaneously.

'Didn't look like nothing from where I was standing,' Perry said. 'You all right, Von?' he added, turning to her.

'I'm fine,' she said. 'I just need to finish up here.'

She busied herself transferring the last few used champagne flutes on the table to her tray, avoiding both men's gazes. Even so she suspected that above her head some sort of silent battle of wills was taking place. And when Pierson turned away and headed outside without another word, she knew who'd won.

'Leave that,' Perry said, placing a proprietorial hand on her shoulder. 'I'll get someone else to do it.'

'Are you sure?'

She realised her hands were shaking. When Perry explained that he'd been on his way to find her anyway to show her where she'd be sleeping that night she felt suddenly, stupidly grateful. So much so that as they crossed the courtyard she found herself confessing that in fact, Russ Pierson had been right. She did have something of his. She just wasn't ready to give it back yet.

'Are you going to tell me what it is?'

Why not, she thought. She couldn't speak about Phoebe to anyone else. Perry had known her, albeit superficially. And he knew the story so there was no need to explain anything. It was Phoebe's last letter to Russ, she said. She needed to keep it longer and read it through. There was something in it that was puzzling her.

'Have you got it with you?'

They were walking by the river now, and there was very little light. She shook her head.

'Where the hell is this place I'm staying?' she said.

Perry gave a desultory wave somewhere off to the right. It was called Neville House, he said. Though everyone called it the Hermitage because it was so far away from everywhere else. He hadn't been able to find her a room anywhere nearer to the college hub, he said, because of the conference.

'Anyway, we're here now,' he said, stopping at a shadowy entrance. 'Follow me.'

Outside the door to her room he held out the key. But as she went to take it he withdrew his hand.

'You know,' he said. 'You were always one of those girls who thought too much.'

'I didn't think that was actually possible,' she said.

'Trust me, it is. That Phoebe business, for instance,' he said. 'It's all a long time ago now. You really ought to let it go.'

'Believe me, I wish I could,' she said. 'But the way she died still haunts me to this day.'

There was a gleam of sympathy in Perry's eyes. He spoke quietly. When he'd been getting the room ready for her, he said, he'd taken the liberty of slipping half a bottle of malt inside. After the day they'd both had they could both probably do with a drink.

Vonny was torn. She was tired after her long day. But the idea of a tot or two of whisky was a strong draw. And it would be nice to have a bit of company.

'Okay,' she said. 'You're on.'

Perry unlocked the door. She'd been expecting a sparsely furnished box. But what greeted her as, with the help of a barely noticeable nudge from behind, she stumbled over the threshold, was something else altogether.

5

'Flowers? Fairy lights? What the hell is this, Perry?'

This was a massive upgrade on her previous room. Besides the floral arrangement and the string lights garlanding the mirror, a tray had been set out on the dressing table next to the bed. Laid out on it Vonny recognised the kind of crystal decanter and glasses usually reserved for the top table at formal dinners.

'When you said half a bottle of whisky I assumed you meant supermarket own brand and a couple of tooth mugs,' she said. 'How did you manage to smuggle these ones out?'

'I thought you needed de-stressing,' he said. 'I know it's not been easy for you, being back here.'

Perry unstopped the decanter and began to pour the whisky. With nothing to do but wait for her drink, Vonny perched on the edge of the bed, glad to take the weight off her feet.

'What happened to you, Vonny?' he said, as he poured. 'You used to be such a confident person.'

'I guess life just didn't turn out like I hoped it would,' she said. 'Though I've only myself to blame.'

'Well, if you want to talk.' He held out the glass and she took it gratefully. 'I'm a good listener, remember,' he said.

'Where do I begin?'

'You could start with why you got sent down all those years ago.'

It only took a couple of sips of whisky to loosen her tongue. Suddenly she found herself plunging into the story of what she'd done to make her lose her place at St Rita's. Predictably, Perry thought the idea of her taking a hammer to Russ Pierson's computer was the funniest thing he'd heard in a long while.

'No wonder he looked so pleased to see you earlier. Not.'

She grinned, weakly. She didn't want to talk about Russ. She was still confused by the business with the letter.

'Trouble with you is you thought he

was better than you. Not just him. But her too. Phoebe Flyte.'

'Phoebe *was* better than me,' Vonny said.

Perry rolled his eyes.

'Pardon me, but you're wrong there,' he said. 'She might have looked like butter wouldn't melt, but it was all show.'

Vonny suddenly didn't feel like drinking any more whisky.

'If you don't mind, I don't really want to talk about Phoebe,' she said, replacing her glass on the tray. 'She was my best friend and I still miss her.'

He was sorry, he said. The last thing he wanted to do was upset her.

'I like you, Vonny,' he said. 'I always have, you must know that.'

He reached over and covered her hand with his. It was big, paw like, and she didn't want it there. What was it with men, Vonny thought, that conversation always came down to this?

'I think you should go, Perry,' she said, attempting to shake it off. 'I think we've got our wires crossed somewhere.'

The weight of his hand on hers grew

heavier. In a split second his expression had gone from tender to hard.

'Oh, you think so, do you?'

'Please, Perry. Come on. Make nice,' she said.

What happened next, happened quickly. Perry had been sitting on the only chair, by the dressing table on which the tray had been set. His leaned towards her, his breath hot and sour in her face. Vonny jumped off the bed and pushed him away.

But for a heavy man, he was quick. Now he was on his feet too, putting his hands on her, shouting. His words were unpleasant. None of it was language she hadn't heard before. The gist of it was that she should be glad that someone was taking an interest in her and that she had no right to refuse him after everything he'd done for her.

He went for her then, pushing her down on the bed. Her entire body was screaming 'No' when her gaze fell on the whisky decanter just inches away from her hand. Somehow she managed to dodge his grasp and, reaching past him she grabbed hold of it and brought it down on his head. She gave him a push and he slid to the ground, whereupon she leaped up off the bed.

She didn't want to look at what she'd done. She simply grabbed the door key that Perry had casually dropped on the dressing table when he'd come in, picked up her bag and ran to the door. Once on the other side she locked it firmly behind her. There was no way he'd be leaving there in a hurry, she decided.

★   ★   ★

She didn't know what made her ring Naomi. Perhaps, subconsciously, it was something to do with the fact that this wasn't the first time she'd carried out an act of violence inside St Rita's College. She had history. Add her attack on a well-respected college porter to her destruction of an eminent professor's computer, then couple it with her most recent act of aggression on Russ Pierson and — well — the runes didn't look too good for her.

But at least Naomi had heard her side of the story. And she must have felt some sympathy towards her. Otherwise, why on earth would she have bothered to ring Vonny up and ask after her wellbeing the other night?

As soon as she'd explained what she'd done and why, Naomi's calm reaction over the phone told her she'd done the right thing. She was on her way, she said. Whatever she did, Vonny was to go nowhere near that door.

'But what if I've killed him?'

'The police will be there in minutes. And an ambulance. Just stay put.'

'You've called the police on me?' Panic began to rise within her.

'The police are coming for Connor, not you,' Naomi replied. 'Perry Connor is the man they've been looking for regarding a string of sex attacks on women in Oxford.'

'No!'

'You must have heard about it.'

Vonny didn't listen to the local news, she said.

'Nothing ever happens round these parts,' she added. 'Though admittedly I may have got that wrong this time.'

'You're such a cool customer, Vonny,' Naomi said.

And that's when Vonny passed out.

★   ★   ★

Vonny lay in her own bed at home trying to process the events of the evening. She remembered being picked up off the floor and checked over by a rather good-looking paramedic before being whisked away in a police car to make a statement, then being driven home by Naomi who, despite Vonny's protestations had insisted on sleeping downstairs on the couch.

If truth be known, Vonny's protestations had been very much on the mild side. It was actually quite comforting to think there was someone close by making sure she was safe. Although the person guilty of endangering her safety in the first place was, according to the detective who'd inter-viewed her, safely under lock and key.

As far as she was concerned, both Perry and her job were history. She was going to have to explain to the Job Centre why she'd jacked it in after such a short time and no doubt she'd be punished for it. But she'd worry about that when it happened.

Right now, she had something more pressing on her mind. As tired as she was when she got home, she'd found herself reaching for Phoebe's letter to Russ again. Nothing in it fitted with the interpretation she'd come up with all those years ago. Namely, that Phoebe was a victim of a man who held some kind of power over her and of whom she was afraid.

Quite the opposite in fact. The confident light-hearted tone of her letter reflected exactly her mood that last night in the Union bar. What if Vonny had simply twisted the evidence because it suited her to cast Russ Pierson in the role of villain who'd rather murder Phoebe than allow her to go her own way? And that once this interpretation was cast in stone, she'd continued to deny all the evidence that the coroner had presented?

Perhaps because Naomi was downstairs, her presence triggered something she'd said the day they'd met in the café. She'd wondered why Phoebe's parents hadn't made more of a fuss at the inquest when the coroner had given her verdict. Vonny had given her usual answer — that they thought Vonny's testament wasn't worth paying any heed to. But what if it was something else? The last thought Vonny had before sleep embraced her was that tomorrow she intended on finding out.

★   ★   ★

Vonny was up early, grateful there was no sign of Naomi apart from a scrawled message telling her she'd been informed that Perry Connor had been charged with six counts of serious sexual assault with more pending. He would be going down for a long time. Beneath her signature she'd written the name and phone number of a counsellor. Vonny screwed the note up, tossing it in the bin on her way out. She wasn't going to be anybody's victim.

Less than an hour later, she hovered at the bottom of the driveway that led to the Flytes' house — if, that was, they even lived here anymore. For all she knew Phoebe's parents could be dead, in which case she'd come on a wild goose chase.

Summoning her courage, she took a deep breath and marched right up to the front door where she knocked hard on the brass knocker. After a long wait, during which time she almost gave up hope of anyone answering, the door opened.

She recognised Phoebe's mother at once. She seemed smaller, frailer and time had etched deep lines on her face. But the inquisitorial set of her head and those scrutinising grey eyes were exactly how she remembered them. Only this time they held no fear for her.

'I'm Vonny,' she said. 'Remember me? Phoebe's friend.'

Vonny had been imagining all sorts of reactions on Mrs Flyte's part to her turning up so unexpectedly after all these years. Anything from disbelief and shock through to abuse and threats to call the police. But not for one second had she expected the reaction she *did* get.

'I've been half expecting you,' Mrs Flyte replied.

Twenty minutes later, they were drinking tea in the Flytes' overstuffed, high-ceilinged sitting room. While Vonny sat awkwardly contemplating the wilderness that was the back garden through the French windows, Mrs Flyte kept up a constant stream of chatter that Vonny could only put down to nerves.

How did Vonny take her tea? She was sorry she had no biscuits but she had to watch her sugar intake these days and they were such a temptation, weren't they? On and on she went until finally she ran out of things to say. Then it was Vonny's opportunity to finally speak.

'How did you know I was back in Oxford?' she said.

'It's a small place,' she said. 'Word gets around. And we have people in common.'

'Really?'

They hardly moved in the same social circles.

'Russ Pierson called me.'

Mrs Flyte stared down at her cup, stirring the contents languidly.

'Him. Of course.'

'You chose the wrong person to be angry with, Vonny,' Mrs Flyte said. 'Russ only ever wanted the best for my daughter.'

She set her cup and saucer down on the small coffee table by her side. 'If you're looking for someone to blame regarding Phoebe's death, then look no further.'

She placed her gnarled hand over her heart and her rheumy eyes filled with tears.

'Yes, I think I'd already come to that conclusion,' Vonny said.

It had only taken her the best part of twenty years.

'I need to tell you what happened the last time I saw Phoebe,' Mrs Flyte said. 'It was my birthday, and the family were round for drinks. Phoebe was late so I was already angry with her when she finally turned up.'

When she finally had arrived she'd been elated, full of confidence, she said. Half an hour into the celebrations, before the cake was cut, she announced that she was leaving college. It had been a terrible blow, Mrs Flyte said.

'And so I did what I'd always done. I humiliated my beautiful little girl in front of the rest of my family. Pointed out how many more times she'd started something and failed to stick at it. Told her she'd always been a disappointment and that no doubt she'd continue to be one.'

Vonny could imagine how humiliated Phoebe would have felt at this public dressing down.

'Did nobody come to her aid?' she said. 'What about her father? Her brothers and sisters?'

Mrs Flyte shook her head. 'They wouldn't have had the nerve,' she said. 'I was a tyrant back in those days.' She held out her wrinkled hands and examined her stiff blue veins and brown age spots. 'When I clicked my fingers, every one of them jumped. Look at me now. I'm powerless.'

She'd always treated Phoebe as the weak one in the family, she continued. Judged her when — unlike the rest of the family — she found things hard at school.

'That night, Phoebe stood up to me. She took on everything I believed in — everything this family was — and trashed it. She was brilliant, though of course I didn't think so at the time. It was my birthday bash and she was ruining it.'

How utterly selfish and insensitive she'd been, she went on. But she'd learned her lesson. Since the moment Phoebe walked out of the family home, having made the decision that she just couldn't make life work so she might as well end it, she — her mother — had had the rest of hers to realise just how special her daughter had been and how she had messed up. Not just that relationship, either. One by one, the other children had drifted away from her. She rarely saw them now, or the grandchildren either.

'My husband walked out on me too. A year to the day that Phoebe died,' she said. 'He'd had enough of living with a woman who refused to own up to the truth. That Phoebe's death was my fault, one hundred per cent.'

Vonny had come here to pour vitriol on this woman. But she didn't need it. She was already steeped in self-loathing. It was odd, but her initial feelings of revulsion were slowly turning to pity.

'I've lived with my shame and my guilt all these years,' she said. 'If I could just take Phoebe in my arms and tell her how proud I am of her for being her own person, instead of my clone.'

'I'm sorry,' Vonny muttered.

'Don't be,' the old woman said. 'I don't deserve your kindness. Or your pity. I took your friend away and blighted your life too.'

She'd heard Vonny's story from Russ, she said. A bright girl like her should never have been sent down. She could have stopped it, but she was too frozen to do anything, she said.

'It was a long time ago,' Vonny said.

'Do you miss it? Academic life?'

'Yes.'

Vonny had taken herself by surprise by her unexpected answer. But no one had ever asked her this question before. And she'd never dared to ask it of herself. Somewhere along the line, she must have decided it was far better to close down that part of her. Ambitions were for people who deserved it.

'I'd like to help you if you'd let me,' the old lady said.

'How do you mean?'

She owed Vonny, Mrs Flyte said. It was

her fault that Vonny hadn't taken her degree.

'I could help you out financially so you could take up where you left off.'

'You can't swap your dead daughter for another, Mrs Flyte.'

Mrs Flyte flinched at Vonny's harsh words. Why did she always feel compelled to lash out, just as the brush of compassion had touched her?

Vonny put down her cup and saucer, stood up and said goodbye. She'd stayed too long in this house. She had one more visit to make.

★　★　★

'You're right. I do have something of yours.'

Vonny had left a message for Professor Pierson. She needed to see him urgently. Now they sat in front of two cups of coffee in Clowns, round the corner from the bus station.

'How are you?' he said. 'I heard what happened. College is in turmoil. Police everywhere. Reporters. The lot.'

She handed him Phoebe's letter. 'Never mind about me,' she said. 'I owe you an apology.'

He widened his eyes in a gesture that suggested he couldn't believe his ears.

'Just take it, will you,' she said. 'I'm sorry I accused you of pushing Phoebe out of a window. And I'm sorry for destroying your Magnus Opus. I just lost the plot.'

Russ smiled. 'I know. I don't blame you. I was a horrible man back then. Taking advantage of a young woman like Phoebe's vulnerability.'

'I won't argue with that,' said Vonny.

'I should have referred her to the head of department,' he said. 'Instead I encouraged her to fall in love with me. It wouldn't be allowed nowadays. I'd be out on my ear as soon as it got out I was fooling around with one of my tutees.'

Particularly, he added, as he'd been a married man at the time.

'It changed me, you know,' he said, 'Phoebe's death. Up until then I hadn't realised the power I had over students. Nowadays I hope I'm a better teacher, a better husband to my second wife, a good enough father and hopefully a better human being.'

They sat in silence, staring at their coffee cups. Then it was Vonny's turn to speak.

'Phoebe's mother wants to pay for me to get the degree I failed to get first time round,' she said.

'You went to see her?'

Vonny nodded.

'She's a lonely old woman these days,' he said. 'Sometimes I go round and we play cards together. Just to keep her company.'

'I'd have thrived in that family,' Vonny said. 'All those opportunities. The competition.'

'What about your mum?'

Vonny scowled.

'You don't want to know about her,' she said. 'Put it this way. She never rated education much.'

Russ smiled.

'You should take her up on her offer, Vonny.' He said.

She shook her head. She had no

intentions of ever coming back to Oxford, she said.

'There are other universities, you know,' he said, with a withering smile. 'Lucy Cavendish in Cambridge is brilliant for mature women students. I could help you with your application.'

'I'll think about,' she said, standing up. 'But I need to go now. My next bus is due shortly.'

'It's been good to clear the air. Even if it did take twenty years.'

Russ held out his hand. Vonny shook it.

'You know,' he said, as she turned to leave. 'You did me a favour, destroying my computer. That book I was writing back then was truly awful.'

Vonny grinned, raised her hand in a final farewell and made her way outside.

* * *

On the bus back home Vonny had plenty of time to think. She didn't want this life, working in jobs she hated while her brain rotted. She was forty years old and at this rate her life would be over before she achieved anything.

Mrs Flyte's offer felt increasingly beguiling. Moving to Cambridge. Making a new start. Eddie would have loved the idea. He loved adventure and taking risks. Hadn't the trip to Germany proved exactly that? She realised she was thinking about him like someone in the past. And she realised too, as, once off the bus and at the front door, just how much she yearned for him.

Outside the house she rummaged in her bag for her keys. The thought of going back into an empty house made her feel miserable. And when, from somewhere inside, music — Eddie's favourite tune — reached her ears, her eyes filled with tears.

Had she forgotten to turn the radio off this morning, before she left? She inserted the key but before she could turn it the door flew open. And there stood Eddie, beaming, and holding out his arms.

We do hope that you have enjoyed reading this large print book.

Did you know that all of our titles are available for purchase?

We publish a wide range of high quality large print books including:
Romances, Mysteries, Classics
General Fiction
Non Fiction and Westerns

Special interest titles available in large print are:
The Little Oxford Dictionary
Music Book, Song Book
Hymn Book, Service Book

Also available from us courtesy of Oxford University Press:
Young Readers' Dictionary
(large print edition)
Young Readers' Thesaurus
(large print edition)

For further information or a free brochure, please contact us at:
Ulverscroft Large Print Books Ltd.,
The Green, Bradgate Road, Anstey,
Leicester, LE7 7FU, England.
Tel: (00 44) **0116 236 4325**
Fax: (00 44) **0116 234 0205**

Other titles in the
Linford Mystery Library:

MURDER GETS AROUND

Robert Sidney Bowen

Murder and mayhem begin innocently enough at the Rankins' cocktail party, where Gerry Barnes and his fiery red-haired girlfriend Paula Grant while away a few carefree hours. There, Gerry meets René DeFoe, who wishes to engage his services as a private investigator, for undisclosed reasons — an assignment Gerry reluctantly accepts. But the next morning, when Gerry enters his office to keep his appointment, he finds René murdered on the premises. He puts his own life at risk as he investigates why a corpse was made of his client . . .

THE FREE TRADERS

Victor Rousseau

The Free Traders deal fur and whisky, debouching their way through the Canadian northern territories. Pitted against them are the country's soldier-police, the Northwest Mounted. Lee Anderson, Royal Canadian Mounted Police sergeant, is on a mission to find a man wanted for murder twenty-five years ago. But when he and a mysterious woman are thrown down a cliff by a dynamite explosion, her memory disappears from the shock, and they find themselves in a wilderness pursued by the Free Traders — who are bent on killing Lee and capturing the woman.

DEATH PAINTS THE PICTURE

Lawrence Lariar

Graphic artist and true-crime buff Homer Bull is always looking for a good murder for his syndicated comic strip. He just never expected to be invited to one — courtesy of his old pal Hugo Shipley. When Shipley himself drops dead from an apparent self-inflicted gunshot wound, it's no laughing matter. Everyone but Homer is quick to accept the suicide bunk. Maybe that's because everyone but Homer has their own sordid secrets and motives. And not one of them is leaving Shipley's isolated estate before Homer finds his friend's killer.

THE LIBRARY MYSTERIES

Steven Fox

Samuel Holmes has just been promoted to lieutenant of detectives when he and his partner Dr. Watson are assigned a high-profile case — the suspected murder of the deputy mayor's son, whose body has been discovered in the library of an exclusive Victorian-era club. But books are also missing, and it's not long before more historical volumes mysteriously disappear from the city's other libraries. As Sam's team search for clues, they unearth disturbing events from thirty years ago that lead them to uncover a web of torture and murder . . .